DARK SUN

New Seattle Book One

M.J. O'SHEA

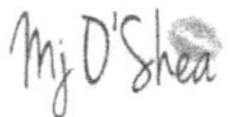

This is a work of fiction. Names, characters, places, and incidents either are the product of the author's imagination or are used fictitiously, and any resemblance to actual persons, living or dead, business establishments, events, or locales is entirely coincidental.

Dark Sun © 2015 by M.J. O'Shea

Cover Art by M.J. O'Shea

Printed in the United States of America

Chapter One

New Seattle 2199

WAR HAD BROKEN out among the triads again; the strongest of the underworld superpowers were pitted against each other for control over the metropolitan jungle of New Seattle.

The people, just like they had been for nearly a hundred years, were ruled by force. None but the oldest — great grandfathers and grandmothers, feeble in their easy chairs —remembered a time when there had been peace.

And daylight.

Lynx Kovalenko sat in the library of his family's estate at Cloud Level, the top of the city, where only the wealthiest citizens were allowed. He idly glanced out the window at the darkness and softly flickering lights.

It had been dark his entire life, longer than that even. Years of pollution had caused a permanent cloud that covered the city and its surroundings and released damaging chemical rains. The upper levels of the city were still beautiful, Lynx reasoned — well maintained and perpetually lit, so that the affluent could still have the illusion of daylight and clean air inside.

In the lower levels of the city, things weren't so shiny and clean.

Midtown wasn't completely horrible, he supposed, just filled with businesses and average-size apartments — working class but acceptable. He'd never choose to live there, and luckily he'd never have to, but the bland existence in the middle levels of the city made his life possible, so he respected it.

That wasn't the case with whatever lived *below*.

Lynx shuddered at the thought of Bottom City, the lowest level of town, so far from the sky that it might as well have been a different planet. Most of the time, Lynx preferred to pretend it wasn't there. He'd never been to the ground, couldn't even fathom the squalor.

Highborn citizens stayed as far from Bottom City as possible. It was an unpleasantness that only the furthest of distances could mask. Dirty and dangerous, the Bottom City was run by the pushers and petty criminals who worked for triads — many of them even for his father, Yuri Kovalenko, the leader of Dragon Triad.

There were dozens of triads in New Seattle, clans and families who'd banded together for business, power...war.

As long as Lynx had been alive, they'd been fighting — Sphinx triad against Chimera, Cobra against Griffin, and most recently his family, the Dragons, had been warring against the Phoenix clan. The two families were powerful and rich. The lesser triads fell in line to serve them. The only choice was allegiance or death.

But that was down below. Lynx never saw the killing from his pristine view at Cloud Level. At least, he hadn't quite yet. Only an unimportant middle son, Lynx had been relegated to the same status as his cousins, the twins Castor and Pollux, and put in training. Together, they'd learned to fight, kill, spy, and everything else they would need to know, so they could kowtow correctly someday to his older brother Leo's every whim.

Bitter much?

Lynx chuckled sourly to himself as he tried to give his attention back to the neglected book on his lap. He hated his status as not quite much of anything. Hated most that there was nothing he could do about it.

A soft overhead chime sounded, alerting him that someone else was entering the library.

Please. Anyone but mother.

His mother been dragging him to every acceptable social function for days, trying to get him to let go of his funk over a recent break up with an opera dancer named Celeste.

Unfortunately, acceptable meant bland and yet somehow full of pressure, rooms of virginal girls and their overbearing society mammas, hoping to make a good match.

Those parties were a lethal combination of boredom, acute enough to make Lynx want to retch, and terror from the circling mother sharks. He would do anything to avoid another one of them.

Luckily, though, it wasn't his mother at the door but his twin cousins, Castor and Pollux. Lynx knew his mother looked down on the twins. Their own mother had come from lesser Midtown, and she blamed that lesser half of the boys lineage for their drinking, partying, and the sexually indiscriminate revolving door that seemed to be a permanent fixture at their apartment.

Lynx thought they were fun but understood his mother's misgivings about their behavior — even though he usually chose to ignore her prejudice. The twins mother came from one of the uppermost levels of Midtown. It wasn't really *that* bad.

"What you up to tonight, cuz?" Castor's wild spikes of gingery hair stood out from a freckled face.

The twins were a near perfect split of their mother's freckly strawberry blonde and their father's side of the coin, the Kovalenko pale clear skin and fire red hair.

"Just reading."

"Oh, *get* up. You are not going to spend the night in a fucking library. It's Saturday, for shit's sake. We won't let you be that big of a loser."

Lynx chuckled at Pollux's blunt statement. He'd always been the quieter of the two, usually letting Castor blab away while he watched with a smile. When he did speak, it was often right to the point.

"Thanks for the concern, guys, but I'm not up to playing nice at some party while all of the social climbers from Metrolevel try to cling to me." He rolled his eyes. "I really don't want to run into Celeste anyway."

Castor grinned. "You won't be seeing Celeste where we're headed."

"You're not going to Tor's party?"

He'd been invited to what was being hailed as the most important social event of the month, but he'd quickly declined.

There wasn't anything that sounded worse to him than hours of increasingly drunk and snarky chitchat — in the best and most expensive of clubs and apartments, of course — that would turn into even drunker public groping and *ugh*.

"*Hell* to the no, we're not going to that lame-ass excuse for a party. We already went for, like, five seconds and left.

Nothing there but a bunch of cranked-out socialites, looking for the richest guy to screw. Same ol' shit as always."

Lynx was relieved. He wasn't going to be up for that scene again for months. If ever. Social jousting with the city's elite hadn't really been his favorite activity in the first place. He'd managed to avoid it completely, until Celeste had started dragging him to all the 'best of the best' events. Still, he felt bad, hearing Castor's cutting summary.

"Those people are your friends, Cas," he admonished quietly. He didn't like them much either, but they were the only people decent society had to offer. Might as well be tolerant.

Castor made a scoffing noise. "Nobody's really friends up here. It's all just politics and sex and, of course, money. That's why they love you so much. You've got that shiny expensive Dragon Prince aura about you."

Fuck lot of good that supposed shiny aura did.

Lynx stopped himself from thinking yet another morose thought about the fickle Celeste.

"So, Lynx, get ready. You're coming with us."

Lynx rolled his eyes but stood ready to humor them. "And where is it we'll be going if not to Tor's party?"

"To the bottom, of course. It's where all the *real* parties are."

The bottom? Bottom *City.* Lynx choked and plunked back down on the buttery antique leather wingchair he'd been lounging on.

"Are you insane? We can't go *there.*"

"We can do whatever we want." Castor was annoyingly assured. He was also, mostly, right. The twins did whatever they damn well pleased. Lynx, on the other hand, had appearances to maintain. He didn't know how to turn them down.

"It's not a good idea," he settled on. Weak, but true.

"Says who? We've been down there lots of times. It's nice to get out of our boring stick-up-the-ass social scene every once in a while."

He had a point.

"I mean, seriously, I was at a party last week where the girl wouldn't serve any colored food or drinks because she didn't want to get anything on her perfect white furniture or perfect white carpet. I'm honestly surprised she let either one of us in."

Lynx chuckled. He'd met a few hostesses that uptight himself.

"Eh, it's just cause we have the best drugs. Everyone knows that." Pollux shrugged.

Lynx nearly choked. "You guys sell drugs?"

If he had any cool points with his cousins, they were circling the drain moment by moment.

Pollux snorted. "Yeah. You think your father is ever going to pay us well enough to actually have some fun every once in a while?" His eyebrow was raised, like he dared Lynx to judge them for it.

"Yeah, right. And we don't have your cushy little trust fund," Castor agreed and shrugged. "Besides, it's easy money. Buy it in Bottom City. Sell it for three times as much up here."

"And that's why you guys go down there — to buy drugs?" Lynx had a hard time even spitting it out.

"That and other things. Anything you want is for sale down in the bottom. *Anything*." Castor gave Lynx a sly smile. He didn't have to bother elaborating.

"I'm not going down there. It's disgusting." Lynx couldn't help it. He wrinkled his nose up and made a face.

"And you know this how?" Pollux, the quiet one, spoke

up again. He looked like he was about ready to laugh at his far too uptight cousin.

"*Everybody* knows."

"But you won't *really* know unless you try, cousin. Put your party shoes on. We're leaving."

"I can't go with you."

Castor rolled his eyes. "Don't you ever want to get out of this place?"

"I've been out. Lots of times." On lavish trips past the borders of the city, past where the darkness dissipated, where the sun was still real and hot and his name and Dragon affiliation meant nothing. He hadn't been all that impressed by the dirt and grime and realness. "It's nicer up here."

"Pfft." Castor reached out and grabbed Lynx's arm.

Lynx could technically pitch a fit about it if he so chose. He decided not to.

And that's how Lynx ended up on one of the Kovalekno family's private lifts, plummeting toward the dirt and squalor of Bottom City in search of wilder entertainments than any of them could hope to find on any of the civilized levels of New Seattle.

Lynx had to admit he was a bit scared.

He was the son of a leader, yes, but a laser pistol could slice him open just as easily as anyone else. And most likely down where they were going, a place he could barely contemplate without a shudder, he'd be a target. His hair and face and clothing would point to him and his money more loudly than any bright flashing sign.

This is an awful idea.

But his cousins weren't going to take no for an answer. He'd been able to tell that right away. It was far easier to go with them for a short while then make his excuses and head back up to where he belonged.

Besides, they were constantly saying he spent too much time moping over Celeste, and that he needed to do something, anything, to get her out of his mind.

It still hurt when he thought about how she'd casually chosen Gem Arturis over him, just because Gem was a first son and could buy her a huge apartment right beneath the clouds. Gem didn't love her like he did; he wouldn't spend all of his time trying to make her happy, or listen to her stories about the theater and...and he was doing it.

Moping. Again.

Perhaps a little adventure beyond the pale *would* be good for him.

Then again, perhaps they'd all be in a detention cell somewhere come morning.

Or dead.

"ARE you sure this is a good idea, guys? If my father finds out..."

Castor made a mocking face. "Loyal little papa's boy. Always worrying about making waves."

Lynx glared at him sourly for a second. "You'd worry about it too if nothing you ever did was good enough."

"Classic middle son angst. Not respected like the oldest, not spoiled like the baby."

"Just ignored — besides, I'm not only worried about my father. What about Marco?"

Their trainer. Castor rolled his eyes. Again. It was one of his most-used facial expressions.

"Marco can bite me. And *you*, cousin, you need to have some fun. Here, try one of these."

Castor held his palm out. Lynx gave the small, pale purple pill a skeptical look.

"What is that?"

"Just a little *bump*, cuz. It'll make you feel really, really good. That's all." Pollux gave Lynx his most trustworthy stare, then winked conspiratorially.

"You are insane. I'm not going to take that." Lynx frowned. He wasn't a big fan of drinking. Drugs were the last thing he'd ever considered trying.

"You'll like it." Castor assured him. "Poll and I will take some too. It'll be fun," He rolled his eyes. "Not boring and pretentious, like you usually are."

Castor produced two more of the pills from his zippered pocket and handed one of them to Pollux, who popped it in his mouth and swallowed. Castor followed suit with a grin.

"I'm not *boring*."

Castor and Pollux both looked at him with telling raised eyebrows.

I am boring. No wonder Celeste...shit. Stop it.

Lynx ground his teeth together and held out his hand. "Fine."

He took the pill and placed it on his tongue before he could talk himself out of it. The bitterness was overwhelming, and he nearly spit it out before Pollux handed him a small foil pouch.

"Here, drink this. Should've warned you about the taste."

Lynx downed a mouthful of the thick liquid, which masked the bitter flavor in his mouth. The drink had quite a kick of its own, and Lynx's mouth tingled and went a bit numb from the strength of it.

"What was *that*?"

"Real absinthe. Concentrated." Pollux grinned proudly.

Lynx assumed that his cousin was the chemist behind the moonshine. He tried to control the boring predictable reaction of being horrified by what he'd just had.

Just go with it, Lynx. Try something new.

"You two are —"

He had to shake his head for a second. He forgot what he was going to say. All of a sudden, his skin felt all rushy, like the nerves were opening up and stretching. It was *nice*.

Why didn't I ever try this before?

"Looks like the bump is starting to work." Castor chuckled at his own observation and elbowed his brother in the side. "Maybe this is the night when cousin Lynx finally comes out of that prissy little un-cracked shell of his."

Lynx made a face at Castor. It was true, though. He didn't know what to expect of the night, but he already felt a little less like himself than usual.

"Are we nearly there?"

"Not quite. We're in Midtown – a bit below the stadium level."

Midtown was still acceptable and fairly safe. Not somewhere a Kovalenko would go without a bodyguard, but they went to the stadium often enough for concerts and glider-ball games.

Lynx's stomach fluttered nervously, and for a moment, he considered having his cousins stop the lift so he could get off and go back to Cloud Level. The drugs already seeping into his system, however, told him that home was the last place he wanted to be when he was feeling the way he was.

I can't believe I'm doing this.

The effects of the bump started swirling through his body, building up until it wasn't just his skin that was tingly and open, but everything. An odd burn settled below his stomach, that melty feeling he was getting was almost like being—

Oh God, was that what Pollux meant by good?

Lynx was starting to worry about whether or not he was going to make a public show of just how good he felt when the lift shuddered to a muscular stop at street level. Lynx's stomach lurched.

"We're here!" An excited Castor crowed as he bounded off the lift onto the old, cracked cement street.

Pollux, and then a far more cautious Lynx, followed him out of the lift. Lynx slowly took in an environment he'd only seen on news footage and school holo-films.

Bottom City.

BOTTOM CITY WAS CROWDED and smelly, hot from the vast turbines that powered the nearly half-mile maze of Midtown and Cloud Level above it. The steam was an atmosphere of its own, and Lynx had to cough a few times on his way out of the lift to clear his throat from the uncomfortable thickness.

Every doorway as far as he could see was covered in lights. Moving neon signs obscured by the smog hawked wares or flashed to advertise women, food, or drink to numb the senses. Lynx thought most of them were probably selling a whole lot more than advertised —if one knew the right questions to ask.

The lights blurred and seemed to run together. Lynx turned his head a few times, his eyes unfocused. The streaks of light reminded him of a game. Fascinated, he flipped his head back and forth a few more times and found himself smiling. The lights were pretty, and he wanted to touch them. Lynx lifted his hand, but the colored streaks eluded him.

"Oh, lord. Look at him, Cas."

His cousins chuckled, bringing Lynx out of his trance. He tried to concentrate on their faces, but his eyes kept falling out of focus, and the noises whizzing past him made him want to turn in circles to follow them.

"Lynx. Stay still. Focus on something on the ground for a second. You've got to get used to it."

Lynx looked down and tried to focus on a crack in the cement below him. It was hard, because the crack kept dancing, but eventually it stilled, and he felt a bit of steadiness creep back into his limbs.

"I'm better, I think," he told them.

Lynx lifted his head and practiced focusing, looking past the distracting lights to the people and the buildings and the street.

The crowd was too much. He had to squeeze his eyes closed and try a second time before there was even a chance of being able to see anything other than a dirty pale blur.

Bottom City was overwhelming, full of people he'd never see at Cloud Level. Pale skin from the lack of light — even the healthy artificial light they had up top — and limp, scraggly hair that was a result of little or no vitamins.

The people were smaller and scurried with an intensity that bordered on panic. The faces streaming past him were harsh, with hostile black eyes that seemed to drill into his skull. Lynx flinched back and held his hand up to shield his face. He felt Castor's grip on his shoulder.

"You're fine, cuz. Just keep focusing. Don't freak out."

Easier said than done. Lynx tried to breathe deep, to keep his heart from pounding out of his chest.

He felt the stares, though, from the black, black eyes.

The gazes were stuck on him, burning through his clothes and making his skin heat in hundreds of little uncomfortable hot points.

Oh, God, why wouldn't they stop *staring?*

Lynx tried to focus on the lights again or the ground. Anything to keep from seeing those eyes.

"Why are they looking at us?" He whispered, his breathing rapidly spinning out of control again.

"Because we're different. They're not going to hurt you, Lynx. The people are harmless. It's the ones who look like us that are dangerous."

Dangerous. Bad.

He spun back and forth, his motions wild and dizzying. All he knew was that he had to keep searching the crowd for faces like theirs, so he'd know who he had to run from.

"Lynx, knock it off, you're wigging out. Cas, he needs a drink to calm him down a little. We should head. *Now.*"

Castor nodded. "I thought we'd check out a bar or two, then maybe get outside to see the ruins."

Lynx, who'd been continuously scanning back and forth, looking for danger, stopped to focus on his clearly insane cousin.

"The ruins? You never said a thing about going *outside* of the city."

The ruins weren't the type of place that anyone ever went. Dangerous didn't even go half far enough to describe the kind of trouble that could be found out in the crumbling dead tree-shrouded old city.

If Bottom City was dirty and crowded and hot, the ruins were *uninhabitable.* They were wild, filled with hackers, rebels, and outlaws, people who couldn't blend in with even the seediest of Bottom City dregs. The ruins were lawless, and Lynx wanted no part of them.

"Good idea, Cas. I've always wanted to hit the ruins, see what it's really like out in the wild." Pollux gave his brother a high five.

Lynx was flustered and disbelieving. "No wait, you guys. *No.* The ruins are dangerous, We could get killed. We *can't.*"

The panic that he'd been trying to suppress rose again in his throat, bitter and hot.

"Lynx, you're tripping again. Think about us. We're all trained in shooting, fighting, and getting out of tough situations. We're dangerous, *your job* is going to be dangerous, and you won't even be doing what you want to do. At least this is *us*, you know? It might be a really stupid idea, but it's ours, and not just some job for the fucking triad."

Lynx considered for a long moment, trying to ignore the black-eyed stares that were still streaming past him. The people in Bottom City would kill them for their clothes alone. He was gladder than ever that he'd brought his laser blade with him.

"Fine."

Castor wasn't going to be talked out of it. If there was nothing that twenty years of experience had taught him about his cousin, it was the fact that he was the most stubborn bastard in New Seattle. Lynx had no desire to try and get back to Cloud Level on his own, so whether he wanted to or not, he was following.

"Do you even know where the hell you're going?"

"Yeah, I heard you go out by the floating market, and there's a bridge that takes you to the ruins. Part of an old highway, I think."

"You heard? That's not very reassuring." Lynx squeezed his eyes shut and took one steadying breath. "Lead on, cousin. And if we die doing this...I'm going to kill you."

Castor laughed. "Let's go."

THE STREETS SEEMED to swallow them whole. People swarmed them, and the smells, colors, and the ever-present steam surrounded them. Lynx felt himself getting sweaty. The air stuck to his skin, uncomfortable and stinging. It had to be dirty.

He had no idea how the Bottom City dwellers stood life every single day in the chemical-laden, soupy fog. Castor and Pollux were scampering ahead of him, familiar with the myriad of people, sights, smells, and sounds.

The drugs swirled through Lynx's blood, stronger and stronger. He was getting used to the feeling, but he had to concentrate on Castor's brilliant ginger hair bouncing through the crowd or else he would get hopelessly lost. His cousins slipped even further ahead, weaving through the people and the steam and the vendors hocking simu-fruits and digital enhancers.

Lynx finally had to stop for a moment, dizzy and nauseated from the people and the smells and the strength of his high. It passed, but by the time he lifted his head, his cousins were gone.

Mother-fucking shit.

Lynx started to circle the area where he'd last seen his cousins. He thought they couldn't have gotten far, but the streets all looked the same, and the stream of black-eyed bottom feeders circled closer, smelling the cloth of his pollution-resistant tunic and feeling his soft, well-conditioned hair and skin. Lynx tried to be gentle, pushing off the people with patient hands instead of revealing the panic he was spiraling into. He was disoriented, foggy, and the lights and people and noise and constant steam weren't helping his condition.

Find a bridge. There's a bridge that crosses the lake into the ruins.

Lynx concentrated on that vague idea. He squeezed his eyes closed, but that made him sway dizzily. He opened them and looked at the ground again, willing it to stay still long enough for him to catch his balance.

I have to find a bridge.

It didn't occur to him to sit still and wait for his cousins to return. He felt like the only thing he could do to keep from spinning into blurry wisps of nothing was to walk. The lights made little swirling patterns on the sides of the late-night shops, the unseen stars displayed in bright unnatural colors that ran together in long, dizzying streaks.

Lynx regarded them blearily but kept walking, staring at doors and lights and faces and the dark creepy eyes that he couldn't escape from.

Ohhh. Lynx could feel it. He was freaking out again. Time to stop and look at the ground again. It was easier if he focused on the ground. So much easier.

He walked again, his gaze on the ground, the gray pebbly concrete flowed river-swift. He felt like his feet barely touched it. After miles and miles of concrete had passed under his slow moving feet (or maybe only a few blocks. It was really so very hard to tell), Lynx smelled what had to be water; its nauseating rankness was different than any of the myriad of smells he'd already encountered.

Maybe there's a bridge here.

Even as that one hopeful thought slipped through his brain, he held his breath, trying to escape from the fetid smell of the water. It was one he hoped he'd never experience again. The stench was thick with dying fish and garbage, heated by the constant steam of Bottom City and teeming with the sounds of a chaotic thriving, multicultural market. Lynx thought of the market up at Cloud Level, with its pristine floors and polite vendors organized into perfect rows of square stalls.

He squeezed his eyes shut as he tried to imagine he was there, among the order and cleanliness. It nearly worked. However, no amount of visualizing would get rid of the smell.

Lynx gagged in the back of his throat.

He noticed a few of the vendors eyeing him with distinct interest. He racked his mind, going through his training and every single maneuver he had learned with the laser blade.

I'm not ready, he realized. *I'm not ready to be a killer.*

He was scared, and the bottom dwellers were shifting inward, staring at him through the huge chunks of shimmering obsidian lodged in their puffy melting marshmallow faces that seemed to glow in the obscene neon steam. They were getting closer, closer...

He thought he saw one of them pull a shock loop from his pocket. The kind that would leave him on the ground and stunned, unable to defend himself.

Screw this. I'd rather look stupid and get in trouble than die.

Lynx picked up his pace and started to look around for a bar, a restaurant, anywhere even partly safe, where he could sit until the waves of dizziness had passed.

He stumbled into a doorway that looked perhaps a bit less foreboding than the others before it had. The door had a common digital reader by the handle. Lynx had seen many like it before.

He stuck his finger into the slot so it could test him for

substances. Readers just like it were all over New Seattle. They checked for enhancing drugs or subdermal weapons, anything that could make the candidate for entry dangerous or reckless. There was a sharp bite for a moment as the machine took a reading of his skin. The light flashed yellow, and a short readout was displayed — it said that he tested positive for mind-altering drugs, but nothing dangerous that would cause him to be refused entry. Lynx breathed a sigh of relief.

Chapter Two

THE DOOR SNICKED open with the dry whisper of hydraulics, and he moved through it into a pulsing purple den filled to the brim with sweating halfway-clothed men and women, slick and shiny, weaving in and out of the crowd.

They weren't the pale black-eyed bottom dwellers, but rather, those like him, out looking for a night that couldn't be found in the levels above.

Right in front of him, a man removed another man's shirt and leaned over, sucking a nipple into his mouth. A half-dressed woman slithered between them, cupping both men's crotches with greedy-seeking hands. Lynx's eyes nearly bugged out of his skull. In his normal state, the spectacle before him wouldn't have been much beyond mildly interesting and vaguely distasteful.

That night, with the bump sliding through his veins, it made his blood boil.

The chaos, the sweat, the heat emanating from rubbing slick flesh... He felt himself harden and had to squeeze his eyes shut to regain control. He didn't want to stick out in a room full of intoxicated people in the middle of Bottom City, so he took a deep calming breath, making sure he didn't sway on his feet, then opened his eyes and looked up at the ceiling to avoid staring at the throbbing pile of skin on the dance floor.

The first thing he noticed was an ornate hanging gold phoenix that dangled only feet from the ceiling — decoration, or perhaps a claim of territory. The sight of it alone made his bowels drop.

Fuck, fuck, fuck! How could I have missed that?

That bird, for him, might as well have been a death knell. Had he seen it right away, he'd have turned and ran, taking his chances with the groping bottom dwellers outside.

He was a Dragon in a Phoenix triad bar. Fuck didn't even start to cover it.

Lynx turned to leave, hoping to get the hell out before he drew attention to himself, but his way was blocked by a rather large man.

"Haven't seen you in here before, boy. You look familiar," The mountain of flesh grumbled.

At least I don't look exactly like my father.

It was probably one of the only times Lynx was glad that he wasn't his older brother.

"I'm here to meet a friend", he said quickly and turned back to slip back the other way.

He blended into the sea of flesh and drew his hood over the signature sunset-colored shock of hair that each member of the Kovalenko clan had a variation of.

Lynx threaded his way through the crowd, hoping to escape the notice of anyone who might recognize his coloring and features, if not his actual face. He'd never been seen in the news, unremarkable second son and all, but to a practiced eye, he'd stand out like a beacon.

Lynx's own eyes were frustratingly unfocused, and he squinted, trying to make sense of the darkness and the flashing lights. He wished more than anything for clarity, sobriety. He was in the one place in New Seattle where he needed to be most alert, and the drugs were still making his head spin.

Lynx moved forward as far into the room as he could go and kept his head down, trying to remain as inconspicuous as a red-headed Kovalenko in a Phoenix bar could be.

He looked up again for a moment to get his bearings and to make sure he'd gone unnoticed. What he saw made his breath catch in his throat.

The lights flashed still, red and purple and dizzying, but they illuminated a man who stood at the bar, surveying the room like he owned it. He was young, probably hovering close to Lynx's twenty, and was obviously high born, with creamy white skin, delicate cheekbones, and big eyes that were showcased on the left side by a delicate swirling tattoo that reached from his hairline all the way down on to his cheekbone.

The boy was beautiful and clearly very rich, not the sort who should be anywhere near Bottom City. Thankfully he lacked the genetically modified sapphire hair that would mark him as a Leonias, the lords of the Phoenix clan.

Lynx had to admit if it hadn't been for that one missing feature, high-ranking Phoenix lord would've been his first guess. The boy's hair, however, was inky black and reflected the lights that swirled overhead as his gaze connected with Lynx's.

He raised his glass and tipped his generous lips in a small beckoning smile.

Lynx felt his pulse race, and suddenly, it was hard to breathe. Never in his life had he wanted something so instantly and completely — and stupidly.

He had to get out.

Lynx headed for a dark corner, a restroom, anyplace where he could hide and hopefully try to locate someone to rescue him. He shoved through the crowd, no longer caring whether or not he was garnering stares.

He ended up breaking out of the edge of the sweating crowd only to stumble into a heavy black curtain. Instead of the solid wall he expected behind the hangings, the curtain parted, and he fell into a chamber, darkened even further than the main room. Lynx struggled to his feet and glanced around in wonder.

The chamber had a sink and long colorful tubes of what Lynx assumed were scented soaps. There was also a velvety soft couch that felt incredible against his easily distracted fingers and a bed that was covered in pillows. A door slid into place behind him, locking.

His stomach dropped. What the hell was happening to him?

And suddenly *he* was there, the boy from the bar outside. Up close, he was even more beautiful, more aristocratic than he'd seemed before. He barely looked like he belonged on earth, let alone a hellhole like a Bottom City bar.

"WHO ARE YOU?" Lynx asked.

A soft manicured finger rested against his lips. "No names."

The mysterious stranger shook his hair from the braid it had been tied in and removed the hooded over-tunic he'd been wearing. The shirt underneath was fine fabric, clingy and expensive. Lynx had been right. He was certainly from someplace far above.

"What are you going to do to me?"

The boy gave Lynx a small smile. "Shouldn't I ask you that? You're the one with the laser knife."

Lynx colored. "I'm not going to hurt you. I got lost. I just wanted to—"

He broke off, realizing how foolish he'd sound if he admitted he was about to call his family. If nothing else, Lynx didn't want to look like a fool.

"You're so beautiful," he whispered, reaching out to trace the tiny intricate lines of the stranger's tattoo.

There goes any chance of not sounding foolish.

He shook his head to clear it. The drugs had loosened his lips for certain.

"Touch me," the young man whispered and took Lynx's hand from his face, slipping it under the sheer fabric of his shirt. His skin was velvety and slightly damp from the heat. Lynx's breath caught in his throat.

"I..." Lynx didn't know what to say.

"Don't you want me?" He touched Lynx's face with those soft slender fingers then drew his shirt over his head, revealing a lithely muscled chest. Lynx choked on a rapid inhalation.

"Yes," he breathed.

It was the truth after all, whether from his own lust or the drugs that circulated through his veins. He'd wanted the gorgeous nymph from the second he saw him.

"Then take me."

The sentence was followed by a kiss — soft lips descending on his, seeking tongue darting out to taste what Lynx had to offer. Lynx groaned and returned the kiss, threading his fingers through the warm silk of black hair. He felt small teeth on his bottom lip.

They bit gently, as if to say *more*.

Lynx cupped the young man's hips and pulled him closer, loving the feel of hard muscle and soft skin against his body. He wanted to feel it without his clothes in the way, skin to skin. They broke apart only long enough to breathe, then returned to the consuming kiss, learning each other's rhythms and tastes. After long minutes, the boy drew away. Lynx felt a moment of chill.

"Hold on."

The boy opened a drawer and produced a tube of some kind of lubricant and then offered Lynx a small black box. For the second time that evening, Lynx blindly stuck his finger out to be sampled. When the box showed perfectly clean results, his lover smiled and stuck his own finger in until a green light and another set of negative results flashed.

Lynx panicked for a moment when a small tube of lubricant was slipped into his grasp. He'd never had his hands on anything so exquisite as the creature in front of him. He'd also never been the type to pick up a stranger, no matter how enticing, no matter how intoxicating his kisses were.

Was he really going to...

"You do know what to do, don't you?"

The boy flashed him a saucy mocking smirk before dropping his loose trousers. The fabric slid over creamy skin until he pooled on the floor and he stepped out of them. His body was perfect, glowing white and flawless. Even his cock was graceful, slender and pretty, white like the rest of him and perfectly shaped.

Lynx gulped and nodded. He did. It was one of the first

lessons that a Dragon was taught, how to love and love well, both women and men. It was a skill they were expected to have.

"So come here, because I want you too."

Lynx needed nothing more than to throw the stranger down and bury himself in the tight heat he knew he'd find within, but he wanted to make it good for his intoxicating unknown lover.

He lifted heavy dark stands from the pale white neck and licked experimentally. His taste was exactly what Lynx had dreamed of...even if he'd never known that he dreamed it.

He felt seeking fingers unbuckling his scabbard and thought for a second that if the boy wanted him dead, after his knife was gone, it would be easy. Lynx gulped and let the knife go, as well as his cloak, tunic, and tight-fitting trousers.

Before his lust-scrambled brain knew what was happening, he was naked and rubbing, flush against the pale perfection before him.

The boy leaned back with a wink and sank to his knees, licking at Lynx's startled erection. He trailed his tongue along the bottom, then pushed the flat of his tongue up against the sensitive spongy skin at the head. Lynx groaned.

"Is that okay?" He asked.

"Yes. Don't stop."

Lynx got another smile before that amazing mouth was back on him, licking, tasting, driving him out of his mind. When he was about to go insane from the teasing, the boy opened his mouth deep and took Lynx in as far as he'd go.

Lynx trembled.

The wet heat, that wicked little tongue massaging him in all the right places -- he tipped his head back and let out a moan. The moan was taken as encouragement. His lover picked up the pace, wrapping a hand around the base of Lynx's shaft and tugging in time with his mouth. Lynx knees started to shake, and the orgasm that he'd been trying to hold back for the past few minutes pulsed insistently at his spine. He tugged on surprisingly muscular shoulders.

"Please, I won't last." Lynx colored.

He knew it was embarrassing to be on the edge after only a few minutes of oral pleasure. He was given an appraising look with those knowing, startlingly violet eyes.

"What did you take?"

"Just some bump. My cousin gave it to me."

"Ahh." A soft smile, and the boy stood. "Then this will be good for you."

Lynx was pushed gently backward until he felt something butt against his calves. He let himself fall until he hit the cushiony velvet covers of the low bed. His black-haired angel crawled over him, rubbing against him with that unbelievably soft skin.

He kissed Lynx again, something that was not expected and with seemingly uncharacteristic shyness. He tasted a bit like Lynx but also like himself, sweet, like cherry, and a bit wild. Whatever the flavor was, Lynx wanted to spend hours exploring it.

Lynx returned the kiss, tasting and loving the silken feel of tongues sliding together. He rubbed his palms down the boy's back until they were cupped around the perfect swell of his round little ass. Lynx sighed and squeezed, dragging the boy closer to his body, as close as he could get without being inside. He wanted to explore every soft nook and cranny, let his hands and tongue feel their fill.

He didn't get a chance.

The boy slithered down his body again, raining little

kisses and bites, sucking on Lynx's nipples and blowing on them. Lynx tried not to cry out like an inexperienced greenling, but his limits were tested again and again. Biting, licking, blowing, tasting long trails, until that deliciously wicked mouth was poised over his straining erection one more time.

"Don't come," his dream lover whispered with a naughty grin before diving back down and engulfing Lynx's shaft in his own brand of hot-wet perfection. Lynx drove his hips up, straining at the edge of release.

"Not yet."

His lover crawled away for a moment, then something warm and slippery was spread on his cock. Just the sensation alone sent him careening once again toward the brink of orgasm. Then the boy straddled Lynx's thighs, guiding with his small hand until Lynx's head breached the tight muscled entrance to his body. He grunted a bit and scrunched up his face but sank determinedly, until he rested flush with Lynx's body.

"You're, ah, bigger than I expected." His sexy nymph grinned breathlessly.

Lynx couldn't form the words to reply.

He was in paradise. Hot, tight paradise — and he was clenching his teeth to keep from coming. The boy leaned over, his long hair slipping to the sides of Lynx's head.

"I've been where you are before. Just let it go. It's okay."

He rolled his hips and tightened interior muscles. Lynx started doing calculations in his head, reciting the birth and death dates of old Dragon leaders, trying desperately to hold on to control. The boy chuckled quietly and started to move, lifting and lowering, leaning over to suck on Lynx's neck.

"You feel good," he whispered and moaned quietly in Lynx's ear.

"You...ahhh." Lynx pushed his hips into the shifting, torturing tightness.

Those same soft fingers that had nimbly divested Lynx of his clothing found his hands and threaded their fingers together in an oddly intimate gesture. They kissed again, and cherry-flavored lips distracted Lynx from the agonizing pleasure below.

"Right there," came another whisper. "Don't stop. You're going to make me come."

That was enough to make Lynx shudder. "Can't....much longer."

"I know."

The tempo increased, and they both began to sweat in the Bottom City heat. Their bodies slid together, slick and dizzyingly fast — almost surreal in the lack of friction. Lynx floated as if in a swimming, swirling bliss, unaware of the room around him, the sounds of the club outside. Nothing was real other than the heat and the consuming slick grasp of his lover's body.

Lynx tried to untangle their fingers and reach for the boy's cock, wanting to bring him the insane pleasure Lynx was feeling, but he was denied by a strong grip.

"No. Like this. Just keep—oh, *God.*"

Lynx could feel the convulsions starting, the boy's tight body massaging, squeezing, and then his belly was splattered with wetness. Lynx arched off the bed as his own climax hit, stronger than he'd ever felt before.

He gripped the boy's hands hard, needing to feel something other than the churning whirlpool of sensation that was pulling him under. He cried out one more time before flopping bonelessly back onto the damp velvet coverlet.

They were silent for long minutes before the intriguing

raven-haired mystery rolled to the side and slung an arm over Lynx's chest.

"You..." Lynx started.

"Shhhh. Just close your eyes for a little while. I'll make sure you get safely to Cloud Level before the morning hours."

Lynx's head spun, and his skin still tingled with fading bliss, but he was exhausted — both from his unexpected night and the wild little lover who was currently sprawled across him.

So he closed his eyes, as directed, and in the middle of a Phoenix bar in dirty, dangerous Bottom City, he passed out.

Chapter Three

ORION LEONIAS WOKE to the blinding light of a simulated sunrise.

Jesus, talk about overkill.

He sat up in his bed and stretched. He'd barely been in bed for two hours, having snuck in after...

Orion flushed.

After.

"Morning, Master Rion," intoned a familiar voice from the speaker box in the hallway.

The door to his chamber slid open with only the quiet, well-mannered hiss of expensive machinery.

"Morning, Sawyer, and I thought we were going to can it with the master stuff. I'm not a little boy anymore."

Not at all, he thought with a smile, savoring the slight pleasurable soreness he felt when he stretched.

He'd surprised himself the night before. It wasn't like he was in the habit of offering his ass to the first attractive guy who looked his way. In, fact he'd never done it before.

There'd just been something about the gorgeous green-eyed Dragon boy — and Orion knew he was a Dragon, probably some low-ranking Kovalenko. His flame-colored hair had left no doubt about that.

Orion hadn't cared.

He hadn't cared the first time, when they'd come together with little more than a sentence or two between them, or the second time in the middle of the night, when the Dragon boy had simply slung Orion's leg over a muscular thigh and sunk into him from behind. Not even the third just hours before, a quick frantic coupling and then a furtive journey to Cloud Level before they were missed, their parting peppered with kisses and touches.

It was a night that Orion wouldn't forget for a long time, even if he knew it shouldn't, *couldn't*, happen again.

What's for breakfast, Sawyer?" Orion asked, eyeing the covered tray hopefully. He'd used up quite a bit of energy on his young Dragon lover.

"Pineapple slices and pancakes."

It was too bad the pineapple was genetically simulated. Orion had had a real slice of pineapple once, one that had been painstakingly grown in a lab down in Midtown. It had been heaven. Even the fake fruit was expensive, though — and packed with vitamins the bottom dwellers bodies couldn't even handle in more than small doses. The difference in his life from theirs made him so angry. Orion sighed.

You haven't even been awake for five minutes. Give it a rest for once.

"No bacon?" He asked.

Even if it hadn't been real bacon in years, it still tasted good, and he craved it when he'd had a bit too much to drink.

"Late night? I can probably find you a few strips if you want to wait for a moment. Oh," Sawyer added, raising his eyebrows at Orion's still dyed hair. "You might want to wash that out. Aries is out in the hallway. He wants to talk to you, and I don't know how you'd explain your sudden change to black. I'm guessing that's a conversation you'd rather avoid."

"You're right. You know what, skip the bacon and please, just stall Aries until I'm done washing off."

Sawyer gave Orion a knowing grin. "Yes, Master Rion."

"Hey, what happened to dropping the master bit? I told you, I'm not a boy anymore. Haven't been for a while."

"You'll always be a boy to me, Master Rion."

And you'll always be my father. At least, more of one than my real father has ever considered being.

Sawyer knew everything there was to know about Orion. He trusted the man implicitly. It didn't mean he was going to share the previous night's Bottom City adventure with him, though. There was such a thing as too much information, after all.

ORION EMERGED from his bath chamber showered, clean, and dreading the talk with his belligerent cousin Aries. Talk about a fitting name. Orion wondered if Aries would've been meeker if perhaps he'd been named — No, he probably would still be that same looking-for-a-fight asshole.

Wonder what he wants to fight about today?

Orion didn't have to wait long to find out. Aries pounded through the open door, which slid noiselessly to a close behind him. He looked frustrated by the lack of something to slam.

"Where the hell were you last night? I was looking for you all over the place."

Orion decided that a version of the truth would be easiest. "I found someone entertaining to pass a few hours with. I didn't want to be disturbed."

Aries made a face but relaxed a bit. "Well, that's understandable, I guess," he mumbled. "Did you go down to that club again?"

Orion nodded.

"Rion, why do you keep going there?" A look flashed over Aries's face, more concerned than anything else.

"It's fine, Aries. I have my private room, I can leave quickly if anything starts. Besides, it's all Midtown and Cloud Level citizens now. They go to the bottom for adventure, but all they see down there is each other." Orion rolled his eyes.

"I just worry about you, kid." Aries ruffled Orion's hair.

"You do?" Orion seriously doubted that.

"Yeah. You might be sophisticated and grown up now, and lord knows, I don't want to know about most of that, but I remember not that long ago when I was teaching you how to shoot a gliderball. I heard there was a Dragon kid in the club last night. That place is dangerous." Aries huffed out a long puff of air. "We'd have had the sucker, but he disappeared. I actually wanted to see if you'd noticed anything."

Orion tried not to smile. "I was there for a few minutes. Didn't see anyone that looked like a Dragon."

Aries made a growly noise. "He was there. You know, it was probably that thief, Yoru Katana, sneaking around and trying to find ways to steal more from us. He got that big shipment of CFC Blockers just a few days ago. You'd think he'd be tired of fucking with us."

It was hard for Orion to act casual. He tried to inject a good amount of scorn into his voice. "There's no way that Yoru Katana is a *Dragon*. What would be in it for him to steal from his own family? They've been hit by him just as many times as we have."

"Well, it doesn't matter. We've moved tonight's shipment from the East Battery Street port. If he had plans to be there, he's going to be a bit annoyed. Especially when he runs into the guards I'm setting out there." Aries grinned.

Orion tried to appear as disinterested as possible when in fact he wanted to scream.

He'd spent days preparing his team to nab that shipment. Now what? He wanted nothing more than to demand information about where the shipment was being moved to but realized it would be stupid to look so interested and, not to mention, completely out of character for him.

He was, after all, seen as a frivolous decoration for his father — and he was good at playing the role. On the surface at least, Aries did all the real work for the Phoenix triad.

Guess I'll have to find out later.

Orion tugged a comb through his damp hair. Bright sapphire blue and long enough to reach his mid-back. He usually wore it in a single thick braid, out of the way, and dyed it black with some wash-out dye whenever he left Cloud Level. No matter what he was up to, it was never a good idea to announce his high-ranking Phoenix status in the lower levels of the city. The hair color would do just that.

"When are you going to cut that shit off? You look like a girl."

Aries reached out and tugged on a lock of it, yanking hard enough to make it hurt, like he'd been doing since they were children.

"I like it," Orion replied placidly, continuing to brush his hair as it dried. He wanted nothing more than to get his cousin the hell out of there so he could deal with the problem he hadn't seen coming. "I have stuff to do, Aries. Is there anything else?"

"What could you possibly have to do? Message your pretty little friends to meet you for another day of whatever the hell it is you princesses do?"

Aries gave him a long, condescending look, which he was annoyed by, considering how often Aries entertained one of Orion's 'pretty little friends' in his own private suite. They were shallow and silly, but not bad people.

Orion, as usual, used his family's poor opinion of him to his advantage. He put on the most vacant look he could muster and started prattling on about stuff Aries would rather get shot than listen to.

"I have to brush my hair, and it takes at least an hour to pick out what I'm going to wear — then there's makeup and shoes and I have to set up the party for later tonight..."

Orion trailed off and raised his eyebrows at Aries, hoping that he would get the hint. His cousin hesitated, like he thought perhaps it was a bad idea to leave, or maybe he just wanted to stay and pile on more derision. Orion simply continued to brush his hair, trying to look as disinterested and vapid as possible in hopes that his cousin would grow bored and leave. It worked.

"I guess I don't have anything else. But don't just float off somewhere. Katana's been out a lot lately. I can't begin to imagine what he'd do if he got a hold of the likes of you."

With a harrumphing noise, Aries stalked out through the door, which slid, unsatisfying and silent, to a close behind him.

For once, Orion would have loved a satisfying slam.

"WE'VE GOT work to do, guys," Orion announced not an hour later when he burst through the door of his command center in the ruins.

Rumored danger aside, the ruins were where he felt most comfortable, most like himself. He pulled his newly re-dyed black braid from underneath the voluminous hood of his tunic and sat at the multi-screened console that was his information network.

"What's the matter, boss?"

Orion's right hand, Pavo, sat in his chair and looked at the screen array as if there would be some sort of answer there.

"My damn cousin moved the drop location for the ship-ment tonight. I need to find out where it's going."

"There was no way to just ask?"

"Not without looking suspicious. They moved it because of us. Well, because of Katana anyway." Orion grinned.

He loved the rush he got when he slipped out of the role of perfectly made-up society son and into the well-armed and comfortable garb of Katana. Out of his two lives, it was the one he preferred. Vastly.

"So check shipping manifests?"

"What? No. Don't waste your time with that. Even my cousin wouldn't have been that stupid. Try all types of messages, voice calls, check our surveillance footage. Someone said *something* somewhere that will help us."

He shivered. It was cold in the old tree-infested storage shed where Orion and his small gang of followers worked under hacker aliases and the cover of the ruins.

"We've gotta work on getting heat into this place. Last winter was awful."

Even with the sun on the other side of a huge bank of

gunk there was still a difference between winter and the summer out in the non climate-controlled ruins.

"We can probably lift a blast furnace from one of the schools on Metrolevel."

Orion shook his head. The Metrolevel was right beneath Cloud Level, the top of Midtown, and the kids who went there were fairly privileged, but he still felt wrong about it.

"No, not from a school. I'll work on it. But today we deal with the shipment. This one is important."

Pavo nodded. Orion glanced around, noticing for the first time that other than Pavo, the room was empty.

"Where's Seth and Vela?"

"They went to get snacks."

Orion rolled his eyes. "Right now?"

Pavo looked wounded. "What? We didn't know it was emergency new plan time."

Orion sighed. "I know. Let's get going on this. Start searching footage from my Dad's and Aries's offices. I'll go through the recorded voice communication and text messaging."

Orion sat at one of the large computers and pulled up a program that he'd concocted. In short, it could get into anyone's message history, manifests, mail, voice calls, the stuff that wasn't public register.

Most people's actions were automatically uploaded onto the many networks' news feed updates, but only if that person was chipped — and none of the higher-up triad members were. It was one of the reasons Orion was so perfect for what he did.

The other members of his team were chipped, and he and Pavo were constantly forced to come up with new ways to trick the up-loaders so that their movements went unrecorded. Orion was still working on a permanent program so they could broadcast movements all day long and never be anywhere they said they were. He was close, but didn't quite have it yet.

"HEY, Rion, I've got something here on the security footage. It looks like Aries and your uncle James are talking. I can only see Aries's face."

"Can you enhance the footage — get a good read on what he's saying?"

"Yeah, I'll try." Pavo keyed in a sequence of strokes on the screen, bringing the footage of Aries closer and focusing it.

"Can we tell what he's saying?"

"On it already." Pavo punched in another sequence of commands, and the computer's electronic voice replicated Aries's words in a polite mechanical monotone.

"I have a plan, Father. I'm moving the drop to the Crossroads Depot. It's public, not Phoenix or Dragon territory. Nowhere that Katana would look for us."... "No, I didn't tell anyone. Well, Orion knows I moved the drop, but not to where."

His cousin and his uncle turned, walking toward the door and the camera.

"That pampered princess?" his uncle sneered.

The computer voice was still flat, but Orion could see the face his uncle made. He knew the careless socialite was a perfect cover, but it still stung to be reminded of what his family thought about him.

"What on earth would you involve him for?"

"I was just...venting."

"Well, let's hope he doesn't 'vent' to any of his little butterfly friends."

Shit...

That's exactly what Orion had to do, otherwise, his cover was blown. If he was the only one who knew that the shipment had moved and Katana somehow ended up at the new location, he would be toast. At the very least, he'd be closely scrutinized. Scrutiny was the *last* thing he needed.

"Pavo, can you guys handle this one? I've gotta be seen at Cloud Level tonight, or this is going to look really obvious. We can't afford to have anything blow up in our faces right now."

"We got it, boss. Vela and Seth are on their way back right now. It should be fine, low security."

"Just be careful."

"You be careful too. Waltz around in front of at least five cameras, gossip up a storm."

"Don't worry, I will. Shit. I hate this part of it."

The last time Orion had made a public appearance on Cloud Level, his crew had plastered the walls of their hideout with pictures of him made up like a piece of candy. He'd laughed along with them, then pulled the photos down at the first opportunity.

"I'm leaving. It takes forever to get this black stuff out of my hair, and I'm going to have to look nice and pretty tonight."

Pavo grinned and waved him out the door. "*Go.*"

"I'm going, I'm going. Don't forget to message me when you get back. Say 'the dinner party went well, and I'm sorry you had to miss it'."

"What if the dinner party didn't go well?"

"Then I'm sure I'll hear about it soon enough. But it better. I'm counting on you guys. Get the meds. Stay safe."

"We'll be fine, boss. Pretty soon, we won't even need you, and you can go back to a life of constant tea parties and —"

Orion slammed the door to their storage unit and left, grumbling the entire time.

Chapter Four

MONDAY MORNING HURT. A lot. Lynx been asleep most of Sunday and then up all night, thinking about the boy in Bottom City. Currently he was in jujitsu with his cousins and a few other trainees, not his favorite activity on the best of days. He already couldn't wait for it to end, and they were only in the middle of their warm-up routine.

"Hey, Lynx," Castor whispered, glancing around to see if their instructor was watching. They were supposed to be concentrating on their center. Castor had a hard time with that, even when he was undistracted.

"Shhh," Lynx hissed back, not that he had a great respect for the jujitsu class. He just didn't want to talk to his cousin. And his head hurt.

"What happened Saturday night?" Pollux looked up from his stretch with an expectant grin.

At that moment, their instructor called an end to the stretch and told them to rise for sparring. Lynx had never been more grateful for an interruption in his life. He was a bit less grateful that Castor was his assigned sparring partner.

"Combination C. Red group defend, blue attack!" Marco, their instructor, barked out the order.

Lynx was a red that day, the colored sash tied around his belt designating him as a defender. He sighed.

"Ready, begin!" Marco's shout rang through the cavernous training gym.

Castor came at him, performing the prescribed combination of attacks. Lynx easily parried his punches and threw a casual crescent kick to block a low and unexpected punch.

"That's not part of C," Lynx reminded Castor. He was barely out of breath. Castor threw another unscripted punch.

"You're not even trying." Castor was winded, and his redhead complexion was already turning pink. He kicked at the back of Lynx's knee, but the move wasn't controlled, and Lynx easily avoided it, taking Castor by the heel and flipping him down on the ground.

Castor grunted and jumped back up. "Where were you Saturday night?"

"I don't want to talk about it." He spun and blocked yet another of Castor's attempts to get to him. "Hit harder. You're never going to pass the brown belt test with that strike."

"Screw *you*." Castor hit again, harder. Lynx knew it drove his cousin insane that the fighting came so much easier to him when he barely even cared about it. It was a good distraction from the topic, he thought.

"Thanks for ditching me, by the way. That was really mean. I could've gotten killed."

"We didn't mean to."

"Yeah, we came back to look for you as soon as we

noticed, and you were gone." Pollux grunted from a few feet over.

His partner took the opportunity to land a punch right in his gut. Pollux made a stunned choking noise and doubled over. He held his hand up to his partner to signal a break but stayed bent over, breathing slowly. Castor, on the other hand, sped up, trying to get an advantage over him. Like that was gonna happen.

"It still sucked. You guys took off, and I was left down there, totally out of it and barely armed. It would've been on you if I'd ended up skewered by some Phoenix."

"I'm really sorry, cuz. It was an accident, and we felt really bad about it until we found out you'd gotten back in one piece. Hey, if you're not going to tell us where you were, then will you at least tell us who you were with?"

"No one," Lynx lied. "I was alone, fucked up, and wandering around in Bottom City. I finally found a lift and got myself home, no thanks to you two. Discussion over."

He struck out with another kick to Castor's ankle, which he easily then grabbed and pulled until his cousin was once again flipped over and lying flat on his back. Out of view of their instructor, Lynx rammed his knee into Castor's side hard enough to bruise.

"Fuck," Castor muttered, sounding irritated. "That hurt. What's your damn problem?"

"That's for leaving me alone down there." He jammed his knee in once again, pairing it with an elbow right below Castor's jugular. "And that's to remind you that next time you and Pollux want to involve me in one of your dumb schemes, think again." Castor choked a little, and Lynx let up on the pressure.

"Fine. Shit. I said sorry."

Lynx nodded and stood, offering his hand to Castor.

Their trainer clapped his hands, signaling the end of that particular sparring session.

LYNX SLUNK through the quiet streets of Bottom City, trying to stay as far away from touching any surface as he possibly could. The place was far worse than he remembered it from the last time he'd been down here.

It was morning in the city, or what would be morning if there were ever any daylight. As it was, the steamy dirt-crusted streets of the bottom were almost eerie in their dark silence and had that early morning feel that had nothing to do with light or dark and everything to do with the stillness that could only be found when everybody was at home and asleep...well, nearly everyone, at least. Lynx had been wandering for hours.

He'd been looking all over Cloud Level for the black-haired minx who'd never left his consciousness for a moment since that one wild hot night they'd shared days and days before.

At first it was just halfway, a glance at every public place, a scan through the faces at the parties he'd started suffering through in hopes that he'd run into him again. Then his efforts became more concerted. He'd asked around, giving as accurate of a description as he could.

Nothing.

By that point, Lynx would have given anything for a name, another glimpse of the man's face, some kind of connection between them. All he had were half-dark memories of hot sweaty skin and breathy moans and a vague fear that to find the boy again, he'd have to sneak right back into the same Phoenix bar where he was lucky he didn't get killed the first time.

Lynx wasn't paying much attention to the streets around him, only looking for that one familiar doorway that might lead to answers about his mysterious raven-haired lover. He knew he wasn't being very smart. His training with the triad had taught him stealth and circumspect behavior. He was just too distracted to care.

Apparently he was also too distracted to notice the group of teenaged boys who had been creeping closer and closer to him. By the time Lynx noticed the group of adolescent thieves, they were close, crowding his space and withdrawing knives and laser guns, eyes on the cards that mostly likely dangled from his waist in the protective pouch he kept them in.

"Give us your wallet," the leader huskily croaked, his voice scratchy from the constant cold that most bottom dwellers seemed to have.

Lynx decided it was best to bargain, and food usually worked with boys of all ages. "C'mon guys, I'll buy you breakfast. You don't want my cards. You won't even be able to use them."

"Yoru Katana will fix them for us so that we can," the leader bragged quietly.

Yoru Katana would fix them.

Of course he would. It wasn't enough that the bastard was stealing from his family, now he was going to reprogram Lynx's credit cards too? The Dragons had been trying to catch the notorious hacker thief for months, policing the shipping ports, watching the black market for large quantities of stolen meds.

Katana and his cohorts must have had the best contacts in New Seattle to move that much stolen merchandise without detection. It only seemed fitting that he'd be willing to help a new generation of thieves steal from the rich and unaware.

The group of street urchins moved forward. None of them would be menacing on their own, but a group of starving teenagers, some easily the same size as Lynx, suddenly became dangerous. They had their knives out, rusty and antique, and their laser guns were so old, they were probably more likely to explode than shoot him. But the kids were too close for his blast shooter to be effective, and that was the only thing he had with him. *Shit*. He'd managed to get himself in even more trouble than last time.

"Hey, kids. Scatter!" The voice was commanding and loud — and familiar. It itched at the back of Lynx's mind.

"Katana!"

Lynx's heart clunked in his chest. It was Yoru Katana? The thief that nobody ever saw was standing just feet away from him? He seemed small to carry such a heavy load of infamy. Lynx stared as the urchins called excitedly and crowded close to the cloaked figure. He passed out a few packets of something that Lynx couldn't see, then handed them bread and bags of what looked to be simu-vegetables.

If only I can get to him, I'll have my father's respect forever. Lynx clenched the handle of his pistol.

"Take these to your families, and I don't want to see you bothering this man again. He's one of my friends."

Friends? Lynx recoiled. How could he be friends with *that*? He was confused. That was, until the hooded figure lifted his head and smiled.

Oh. My. God. Lynx choked on his gasp. The mystery lover whose soft skin and tight body had kept Lynx up for days dreaming. Oh God, oh god, *oh god*. He was Yoru Katana? Lynx felt like he was going to vomit.

A dark strand of hair escaped from Katana's braid to stick to his face in the ever-present steam. His smile faded as the boys scampered off with their prizes.

"You're *Yoru Katana?*" Lynx didn't know what else to say. As it was, his voice stuck in his throat. The fingers on his gun grew slippery with sweat. He wanted so badly to pull it out, drag the thief up to his father — but he couldn't force his stupid feet to move.

"Take your hand off your gun. You're not going to shoot me."

Lynx did as he was told, his hands shaking. He was angry with himself for not doing what he'd been trained to do, angry with the boy for being something that Lynx had no choice but to hate, angry because no matter what, Katana was still so beautiful that all Lynx wanted to do was kiss him...

"What the hell were you thinking?"

The annoyed voice broke through Lynx's thoughts.

"I can't keep your fool ass alive if you do dumb shit like that."

Lynx was shocked out of his agonizing by the boy's tone of voice. It was nothing like the mysterious soft lover. Instead, it was strong, businesslike, and supremely pissed off.

"Dumb shit like what?" Lynx couldn't help responding with an equally annoyed voice. The contrast between his lover of the other night, pliable and gentle, and the angry outlaw before him stung somehow.

"Bottom City is the most dangerous when it's nearly deserted. Come with me before you run into some real trouble. Those children were nothing compared to what else is out there, and they could have easily taken you down."

"Wait. *You're* Yoru Katana?" Lynx needed to hear him say it out loud. Until then, it would hardly seem real.

"No time for that. We've gotta get you out of here. Those kids will only wait till I'm gone, before they'll go after you again."

"But you told them not to—"

Katana rolled his eyes. "You can't be that sheltered."

Katana snapped a pair of restrainer cuffs on him before Lynx even had a chance to think, then he took a piece of thick cloth from the pocket of his cloak and tied it around Lynx's eyes. Lynx's pistol was neatly removed from his cloak, and he was quickly searched for any other weapons.

"What the hell? I'm not going to do anything to you."

"No offense, but how do I know that? Plus, I can't have anyone seeing how to get to the place where I'm taking you. I don't know who is tapping into your thoughts."

"No one. I don't have a *chip*."

Who does this asshole think I am? No child of a Dra—oh.

He didn't know Lynx was the son of a triad boss. He hadn't meant to be insulting.

"Still...precaution."

"If I did have a chip, what was blindfolding going to do? My updater would've just automatically announced my location to all the networks as soon as we got there."

Katana let out a low chuckle. "There isn't any network access where we're going."

Lynx panicked a little at that but didn't fight. There was no way he was getting out of the restrainer cuffs without their code or a remote, but he needed to get the blindfold off if he was ever going to be able to relay Katana's location to his father.

If I could just get Katana in Dragon custody...

It was going to be such a pain to try to do it with no network coverage. He needed to get to his loc —

"You know, I can hear your little brain scheming, Dragon boy. I'm not going to give up anything that you can use to help your boss."

Boss?

Lynx breathed a small sigh of relief. At least Katana still didn't know who Lynx was. If so, it was likely he'd contact his father for ransom money. That would be the final humiliation, to have his family know he'd allowed himself to be captured.

"Besides, you might want to remember who saved you back there. I could've just let those kids have you. They'd have eaten your pale Cloud Level ass alive."

Lynx grunted in reply. That was a fact he was trying to forget.

He was led through the darkness for what felt like hot, dangerous forever. He tripped numerous times over bricks and curbs and places where the cement had become uneven from wear and years of not being taken care of.

"Where are you taking me? I don't need detailed directions, it would just be nice to know if you're dumping me in Lake Union or something."

Lynx had heard stories of the lake — how years ago it had been blue and covered in boats. Over the years it had turned putrid in the darkness.

"I'm not dumping you in the lake. It's somewhere safe."

"Safe for who?"

"I'm not going to hurt you. Walk."

"I can see you're still a master of words," Lynx grumbled. "Wait, what did you mean back there about keeping me alive? Have you been watching me all morning?"

"No. But it doesn't take long for word to get around that

a clueless Cloud Level citizen is wandering around Bottom City looking to get mugged."

Lynx wasn't sure, but he thought he might have heard soft laughter. He was embarrassed by the fact that he'd acted like an untrained idiot. Right at that moment he tripped, though, and decided it was probably best to concentrate on walking upright.

By the time they finally stopped walking, Lynx felt like he'd been on his feet for a day at least. In reality, it was probably more like a half an hour. He tried to control his sense of the dramatic but sometimes it got the better of him. Even with the blindfold, he hadn't sensed any lights, not even the dim glow from the ever present streetlights that lit the darkness of Bottom City.

He thought they must have entered some kind of tunnel, because the air felt damp, like the steam of the bottom but clammy and colder. Without seeing, there was no way to be sure where he was. He needed to get his bearings, needed to find a way to turn on his locator, needed to —

"Here, you can take this off." Katana untied the bandanna that was around Lynx's eyes and removed the cloth.

"Hey, thanks for the help back there. I never really said anything." Lynx mumbled. Katana grunted "Oh, and thanks for leading me so nicely," he snapped, annoyed that his politeness hadn't been returned. "I could've fallen on my ass easily at least two or three times."

"You spend too much time on Cloud Level. Maybe your eyes need to get used to the dark."

He could sense the scorn in Katana's voice. What, like it was his fault that he was born rich?

"Doesn't look like you've spent too much of your life

down here, either." He shot a pointed look at Katana's perfect skin and manicured hands.

"I haven't."

"Then what are you doing down here now? I don't understand."

"You don't have to. I have my reasons."

Katana's vague answer made Lynx want to scream. What was it with vague answers lately?

"What could your reasoning possibly be, *Yoru Katana?* Take from my family and sell it on the black market for your own gain? For what? You don't need money. Is it just for fun? Real noble."

Lynx wanted to bite his tongue when he realized he'd just given himself up. His anger at being embarrassed by the boy he'd wanted so badly had clouded whatever good judgment he usually had.

"So you *are* a Kovalenko. I guessed it from your hair, but I wasn't sure. Lower-level cousin, stooge of the great Don? There's no way he'd let one of his three perfect Dragon princes wander into Bottom City unattended."

Lynx was offended, but he found his mouth lying, agreeing with Katana's incorrect assumption.

"Yeah, I'm Castor Kovalenko."

"Ahh, one of the twins? I heard you two never did anything without your other half. From the rumors, I'd say you're lucky there haven't been pictures of your escapades in the tabloids."

There *had* been pictures of his cousins in some of the seedier tabloids. Clearly, and luckily, Katana hadn't been paying attention to those. "We obviously do *some* things separately." He blushed when he realized it sounded like he'd been referring to the other night.

"That's too bad." Katana gave him a small smile and said no more.

"Pollux would never be down here," he muttered, feeling the nervous impulse to keep speaking.

It wasn't true. Either of his cousins would probably have jumped at the opportunity to meet such a notorious badass. They'd probably want his autograph or something.

"What is this place?" They had left the darkness of what had, in fact, been a tunnel and entered a small cramped room, nearly as dark and filled to the brim with equipment.

"Best if you don't know, right?"

Lynx looked around at the truly impressive array before him. Flat screen monitors, antique but still useful, covered the walls of the big room, along with security cameras, schedules, anything Katana would need to interfere with the triads' business ventures.

"You really do have everything, don't you?"

"Even a trusty group of followers," came a voice from the doorway. "New recruit?"

Lynx looked up to see a young man enter the room. He had hair a rather startling, and artificial, color of green and eyes like a cat. Katana smiled at him familiarly, and Lynx had to control the urge to growl.

He felt...oddly possessive after their night together. He had to remind himself he had nothing to be possessive about. That he didn't, and absolutely could not want this boy.

You're going to capture him, right? Give him to your father. Forget how it felt to touch all of that white, white skin and be inside of his melting heat.

Lynx bit back a groan and dug his fingernails into his thighs. He was such an idiot.

"No, this isn't a new recruit, Pav. This is Castor Kovalenko. He's paying us a visit."

"Are you nuts? He's a fucking *Dragon*. What the hell is he doing here?"

"Castor can be trusted, can't you?"

Katana gave him a long look. Lynx had the feeling that his balls would be cut off if the answer wasn't yes, so he nodded his head.

"Besides," Katana shrugged. "He's seen our faces but has no way of knowing how to get here, and all he knows is that I'm Katana, and you're—

"Just call me the savior of the people."

"You're an idiot." Katana said it with a smile. "Castor, this is Pavo. He's a good friend."

Lynx nodded. Pavo was a common enough name. It didn't tell him anything. At that point, two more heads popped around the door.

"And this is Seth and Vela."

Seth was a huge tree of a young man, all craggy muscles and not a ton of visible synapse activity. Vela was pixielike, and her hair was arrayed in long hot-pink spikes that were skewed every which way. They both smiled at Lynx, as if visitors were an everyday occurrence.

"I don't get it. I mean, what are you guys?" Lynx was overwhelmed. He didn't know what to ask first but doubted he'd get real answers anyway. He'd seen the way Pavo reacted to him.

"What do you mean?"

"You're this notorious thief. I've never heard that you had accomplices, yet suddenly, here they are, and I saw you *giving* things to those boys. Is that why we can never find any sales of the stolen goods?"

"It's hard to find proof of sales when nothing was ever sold."

Lynx was annoyed by the smugness in Katana's voice. "You've got to be fucking kidding me. You're risking your life, stealing from your *own people*, to give food and medicine to the bottom dwellers like some kind of misguided folk hero?"

Katana glared. "Perhaps I need to put you somewhere where I can't hear you speak until we have time to get you back to where you belong."

Lynx knew he should stop arguing, but he'd never had much luck controlling his unfortunate mouth. "What if you get caught?"

"Oh, I'm sure they'll kill me. The triads would lose all their power if they caught me and let me go."

Lynx couldn't believe how casual he sounded. He was right, though. The triads would kill him without hesitation if he were caught. The thought of that made Lynx's stomach sink.

If I turn him in to my father, he'll die.

"So why are you doing it?"

"Somebody has to, and I'm probably the best candidate." He gestured to himself. "You've noticed that I'm from Cloud Level."

Lynx nodded. It was fairly obvious, after all.

"So, it all makes sense, doesn't it? I'm privileged with *information*, as well as money and all the vitamins, medication, and good food I'll ever need. Who would be in a better position to help people who can't help themselves?"

Lynx still didn't get the point of the whole thing. "You're crazy, aren't you? There's no helping the people on the bottom. Everyone knows that. Listen, are you going to let me out of here now that I've seen your face? I really don't want to get killed. I promise I won't —" Lynx didn't finish. He didn't have the chance.

"Boss! You gotta come look at this. There's another transport, leaving in twenty minutes for the South Sound. Shit *Fuck*. How did I miss this one?"

Katana's attention flashed away from Lynx and toward the computers. "What are they moving?"

"*Solorigine*. It looks like at least thirty units."

"You're *kidding*. Vela, get the bags ready. Pavo, locations and shipping manifests. Get me the transporter number and the stall they're launching from. This one's going to be tight. Seth, pistols, photon rifles, and something short-range. We don't know what we're walking into. Dragon, you're going to have to come with us. I don't trust you here."

"Screw you! I'm *not* going to participate in your insanity."

"No offense. I just want to keep an eye on you until this is over, then you can go back to your slutty brother and your pretty apartment bordello on Cloud Level. You're coming with us — willingly or back in those restrainer cuffs."

Lynx was angrier than he remembered being in a long time, and yet at the same time, a little perversely excited. Stealing from the triads, working with Katana — it should have been the last thing he wanted, but just being near Katana was more of a rush than anything Lynx had felt in his whole life.

"I at least want my pistol. I can cover the back — I doubt any of your guys have better aim than I do."

Prisoner or not, Lynx wasn't going anywhere near that shipping dock unarmed.

"You're not going to shoot anything."

Lynx could've sworn Katana was looking at him with derision. If there was one thing he was tired of, it was being treated like he wasn't good enough. He held out his hand and waited. Finally, Katana dragged the gun out from under his cloak and slapped it into his palm.

"Thank you," Lynx said

"Fine. Let's move."

Chapter Five

THEY'D LEFT the storage unit that functioned as Katana's base of operations and were on the streets of the ruins before Lynx even processed what was happening.

Even if anyone had wanted him to lead them to Katana's hideout, there was no way he would have remembered where it was located. He clutched his pistol and scanned the tumbledown mess that was all that was left of Old Seattle after the war, sure that there would be outlaws in every corner, behind every cracked building and stunted black tree.

"Dragon, this way," Katana hissed, and they headed for what looked to be a storm drain that was covered with brush.

"Where are we going?"

"It's a different tunnel. This one leads into Bottom City and close to the shipping terminals. We're going deep into Phoenix Triad land. You're going to have to cover that hair of yours. A Dragon would draw more attention than all of the rest of us put together. Even as he was speaking, Katana lifted his own hood and clicked something on his wrist.

"What's that?"

"Cloaker, left over from the conflict."

"I can still see you."

"Of course you can -- and so can everyone else. I'll just be ...uninteresting. It sends out a signal that messes with people's perception. When they look at a person wearing it, they see someone unremarkable."

"Does everyone have one?"

"Everyone but you. I said to cover your hair."

"What the hell?" Lynx all of a sudden felt like a big fat target. He supposed that didn't much matter to Katana.

"I don't exactly carry extras. These things are major contraband, close to impossible to procure. Stay close to me, and mine should cover you, at least to a point. Don't do anything stupid. If you give me up, you'll be just as dead as I am. The Phoenix security would love to kill themselves a pretty little Dragon thief."

Lynx glared, annoyed by the fact that Katana was right. He was beyond dead if one of those blue-haired freaks saw him.

They quickly crept through the tunnels. Lynx felt like he tripped over every little crack and bump. It must have been the same way they came in. He'd have to get better at walking in the dark cramped tunnels if he thought he was going to survive the day. He snorted at his own stupidity. Like uneven walkways were even close to the biggest of his problems. Finally, after what seemed like an eternity, they slowed to a stop outside of a rusted metal door with an old valve in the middle. Katana held a small black device with an eyepiece up to the door. He looked and grunted satis-factorily.

"It's through here," Katana whispered. "All of you. Follow me."

. . .

KATANA LED the way through the crowded shipping docks. There were transports hovering, pulling in and out all over the place from what seemed like hundreds of ports. The vehicles moving around on the second-level docks seemed to cut it closer and faster every time they zoomed overhead. Lynx had to stop himself from ducking.

Please let me get through this shit. He wasn't even worried about capturing Katana any longer. He simply wanted to survive.

"We're headed for slot 1-469 B. It's going to be down that aisle right there." Katana gestured toward a busy thoroughfare that was filled with little ground vehicles, whirring every which way on a thin cushion of air and covered in teetering piles of shipping containers.

The vehicles were loaded by efficient android dockworkers, and the humans who ran them punched in directions while clutching digi-pads that were most likely populated by list after list of procedures and checkpoints. Sure enough, the humans weren't paying them any attention. The cloakers were doing their job perfectly. Lynx crowded closer to Katana, just to be sure.

"Dragon, you have your gun?"

"Yes." Lynx checked for his pistol one more time, then refocused on the task ahead.

"Be ready to use it. I don't want to have to drag your body out of here at the end of this."

Lynx pulled out the scarred old fusion pistol he'd been carrying and unlocked the safety. "I'm ready."

They moved through the crowd to the right loading dock, trying to appear unhurried so as not to draw any attention. The cloakers would do their magic, but it was best not to take any chances. Near the end of the aisle, Katana pointed.

"There. Transport ship 907. We need to get into the cargo bay."

"That's me. Batter up," Vela muttered and snuck forward, drawing a black box from her cloak

"Is that some sort of scrambler?" Lynx whispered.

Katana nodded. "She's amazing. With that little eggbeater and her quick brain, she can get us into nearly anywhere. Plus she looks so sweet and innocent; if she gets caught, she can just talk her way out of it — at least she's managed to so far."

Forgetting for a second to be angry, Lynx shook his head in wonder and watched the pink-haired elfin girl pick her way electronically into a thickly secured cargo hold. After a few tense minutes, Vela beckoned at the group, and Katana motioned for the rest of them to join her at the ship.

They crept across the busy cargo bay, trying to blend in and look unimportant. When they were at the ship, they spread out, surrounding the cargo area.

In the newly opened hold stood a stack of cartons all labeled *Solorigine*. The others leaped quietly onto the cargo hold, while Lynx stood by and tried to keep watch with his pistol. His hands were sweating, and he watched the others nervously, trying to get them to move faster. Didn't they know how to *hurry*? He could've sworn he felt the seconds ticking in his head, and the others' footsteps fell slowly on the ramp behind him.

Breathe, Lynx. It's fine.

And it was fine. Katana's team had made quick work of removing the *Solorigine* from the bulky crates. The medicine was all loaded from the ship into neat bags ready for transport. All they needed to do was get the bags and — oh *no*.

A group of men materialized at the end of the aisle from where they were. The men had weapons, and the one out in front had a dark version of the brilliant sapphire hair that the Leonias family had.

Shit. A Phoenix. Even worse, one of the leaders. Lynx's heart dropped to his toes. He gripped his pistol with a shaking hand, not wanting to shoot but sure as hell not willing to die for something that had nothing to do with him. He sure hoped he was ready to kill anyone who got close enough to see his face. It looked like it was going to come to that. The men were drawing closer.

"INCOMING PHOENIXES," Lynx whispered, as loud as he dared. "We need to get the hell out of here."

The others immediately reacted, jumping into warp speed. Bags were hoisted onto the closest ground transport. Vela, Pavo, and Seth hopped onto the idling vehicle and turned it, aiming for the yawning bay door at the far end of the room.

"Run, you guys, *go*. I'll cover you." Katana stayed behind with Lynx guarding him. "Dragon, get out of here."

Lynx went to turn and jump on the transport, but the others had disappeared, zooming off on the near silent vehicle. He turned back, panicking. The blue-haired man and his stooges were sprinting toward them.

"That's Aries Leonias. He's the head of Phoenix security. He can't see me." Katana sounded panicked. Aries had drawn a weapon, ready to fire.

"Stop!" The Phoenix leader cried. "I'll shoot!"

Katana sprinted for the nearest exit, which happened to

be about fifty feet down and closing quickly. Security must have been alerted, because the building was going into lockdown. Lynx fired at Aries as they ran backward toward a hatch in the wall, the only escape still open. Aries stumbled and grabbed his side but kept running.

Lynx turned and tried to sprint, adrenaline and fear raging through his body. He felt his hood slipping off as he ran; the bright red of his hair was surely visible. He hastily pulled it back up.

All of a sudden, Katana jerked ahead of him, like he'd been hit with something, and started to fall. Lynx didn't even think. He sprinted toward Katana, lifted him easily over his shoulder and pushing with every burning muscle that he had -- and some he never knew existed — he ran until they were at the door. He dove for the hatch, pushing Katana in before him, as it too began to close. They slid under, just in time, right before the hatch clanked heavily, connecting with the ground beneath it.

"Give me your fusion pistol," Katana wheezed.

Lynx handed over the old dinosaur of a weapon. Katana held the trigger down, gun right against the seam of the door. Lynx could smell burning metal. Then he aimed the same heat at the door's Open/Close sensor until sparks flew out of the box.

"There. That'll seal it for a while. We gotta move fast, though. They'll break it open soon enough."

Katana handed Lynx his weapon back, then made a face and grabbed at his arm.

"You got *shot.*" Lynx reached for him, and Katana flinched away.

"Yeah. It's fine. We need to get out of here."

They were in some back hallway of the shipping center, poorly lit and winding like a maze.

"Do you know where you're going?" Lynx asked, worried about Katana's arm, the Phoenix security team, and the fact that he might have been seen.

"To a point. I'll come up with something. You should have gone with the others. If I'm caught, there's no way you'll be able to deny being part of this."

Katana looked even paler than usual. Lynx found himself, of all things, worrying about the thief.

"They took off without me. I'm fine, though. Let's move. We need to get you out of here."

"Really? I'm injured, and probably couldn't fight you. It would be easy for you to take me out right now. Or even better — call your Dragon security to haul me away."

Lynx shook his head. "I'm implicated in this. You've made sure of that. Besides," He hesitated. "They'd kill you. I don't want to be responsible for that, no matter how much I hate what you're doing."

"You're serious?"

"Yeah."

"Thank you," Katana said softly, his face sincere. "Let's get out of here."

THE TWO CREPT through the abandoned hallway, conscious of the pounding and sawing that was coming from the hatch at the other end. Soon Aries Leonias and his men would have Katana's hasty welding job broken and they'd be pounding down the hallway after them.

"I think we should take the next doorway. Any place it ends up going would be better than being stuck in this bottleneck if Aries and his men get through that door."

Katana nodded. "I agree. My cloaker wasn't damaged, so it might be some help, but not if everyone's already looking for us. They're not strong enough to convince the brain otherwise when it already knows exactly what it's seeing. Like Aries Leonias and his men. The cloakers didn't work on th — son of a *bitch* that was a set up."

"What do you mean?" Lynx saw another hatch about thirty feet in the distance and started for it, picking up his pace. He was eager to get out of that enclosed hallway.

"The cloakers don't work if someone already knows what they're looking at, and if they didn't work on Aries Leonias, then he knew we were there. The only way he would've known that was if he planned for us to be there."

"So that whole shipment was a trap?" Katana nodded, and Lynx couldn't help grinning. "Didn't work so well, did it?" He had to admit it was kind of fun, tricking the Phoenix leaders.

"Don't get cocky. We're not out of this yet. Get behind me."

"But you're hurt."

"*Dragon...*"

Lynx slipped behind the injured Katana, who held up his hand. He listened for a few moments, then, satisfied by the level of silence, he reached out and touched the sensor that would open the door. The door hissed and opened into an empty room, some sort of industrial kitchen, filled with all sorts of bells and whistles and tubes of things that Lynx had never seen before.

They snuck through the kitchen and the revolving door that led into a cafeteria that would be filled with port workers come lunchtime. It was still just after breakfast, so the place was deserted, as the kitchen before it had been.

"Look, that's an exterior door." Katana pointed toward the far corner. "Let's get out that way and make our way to the closest tunnel entrance."

"How many tunnels are there?"

"Hundreds. The Chimera triad built them between the old city and the new city before the war with the Sphinxes. If you don't know your way around, you could end up in them for days."

They took off at a jog through the empty cafeteria, weaving their way around closely packed tables. They were about halfway through the room when the far door slammed open, and Aries Leonias and his men stormed through.

"Katana!" He shouted, heading right for him and Lynx.

"*Run,*" Lynx hissed and hustled Katana through the door.

He could've sworn he felt Leonias breathing down his neck. He turned once to see the angry Phoenix running after them. Lynx picked up his pace to catch up with Katana.

Once through the door, they stopped for a moment while Katana got his bearings. Lynx didn't have a hope in the world of helping guide them.

"That way," Katana whispered forcefully, pointing toward an alley.

They took off for the cramped alley that ran between a bar and some sort of herbalist.

"Shit, they're coming. In here." Katana shoved Lynx through a doorway.

Suddenly they were running and tumbling down a long set of old wooden stairs. Lynx was glad both of them were on their feet by the time they reached the bottom.

"The door to a tunnel is behind these crates."

Katana dipped behind what looked to Lynx to be a solid row of crates.

"Dragon, *c'mon.*"

They hid behind the crates, silent, and waited, knowing

that Aries and his men weren't far behind. When the men came stomping into the old storeroom, they shrank back even further, crowding the wall. Lynx found himself holding his breath. He could see Aries through some cracks in the crates.

"Where the hell can they be?" Aries's face was beet-red, and he looked like he was about to start stuttering.

"Did you check down the hall, boss? I thought I saw another door that way."

Aries growled at his men. Literally growled. Little bits of spittle clung to his lips, and Lynx had to stop himself from jumping backward.

"Don't just stand here. Go look then! We were so damned close."

The men glanced around the room a few more times, but didn't bother looking behind the crates. Lynx wouldn't have either. The way they were stacked made them look like they were flush with the wall. The men left, followed by a frustrated Aries.

As soon as the men were gone, they turned and sprinted down the tunnel, Lynx following Katana as closely as he could without tripping as they careened through the cramped darkness.

At the end of the long tunnel and after a short sprint from the storm drain, they ran through the doorway of Katana's storage unit hideout, waited until the door was closed securely behind them, and then burst into gales of adrenaline-releasing laughter.

Chapter Six

____

"I CAN'T BELIEVE the look on his *face*," Orion crowed. He was still breathing hard but it was impossible not to smile.

It had been fun to watch his cousin fume — payback for all of those years that Aries had teased him when they were children He knew he was going to hear about it later, but he didn't care. *So* worth it.

"I've never run that fast in my life," Lynx added, panting. "You don't think they saw the way into the tunnel?"

"I doubt it. Hardly anyone knows that entrance is there."

They stood there, breathing hard and smiling at each other. Lynx's face was relaxed, the anger from earlier nearly gone. He looked like he had that night, all sweet and confused, like he didn't quite know what to think.

"Hey, thanks for not turning me in," Orion murmured.

"I can't be the one who gets you killed. I think it'll happen, probably soon, but I don't want it to be me."

"No faith, huh?" Orion couldn't help smiling at him.

As improbable and impossible as they were, cast as their lot had been in life to be nothing more than enemies, he found himself actually liking the sarcastic but honorable Dragon — not to mention that he'd spent days thinking about the way the boy kissed.

God...

THE OTHERS HAD LONG since returned, having dumped the official transport vehicle within Bottom City and stashing the meds in the brush outside the city, where they'd return for it later with their own vehicle. They were waiting patiently in the storage shed. They all surged to their feet when Orion walked in with Lynx.

"I'm fine, guys. Just a little sore," he told them, heading off any concerns. He knew he had to be strong, since he was the leader. It wouldn't do any good to have the others constantly worried about him.

Orion's arm was throbbing, though, and the cloth that he'd tied around it was already tinged pink. It was going to have to be dealt with soon. Pavo gave his arm one quick look and without saying anything dropped what he was carrying and went back into the shed. Orion waited patiently, but he felt a little thump in his chest when he saw the flame-haired Castor Kovalenko leaning against one of the walls of the storage container, exhausted by the aftermath of adrenaline.

Orion had a hard time picturing his Dragon with that name. It didn't seem to fit him, and *he* didn't fit the image that Castor and Pollux Kovalenko had spent their early adulthood cultivating.

The twins were wild, drug dealers, and halfway on the road to being rent boys, despite the money they already had. His Dragon seemed so sweet, like a big puppy. Except when he was in bed. *God. That night.*

Orion still thought of it about a hundred times a day,

and it was much worse with Kovalenko sitting there, looking so beautiful. Orion tried not to notice that even though he hadn't said anything about continuing to keep him captive, Dragon hadn't made a single move to leave.

He was distracted when Pavo came out of the storage unit with a medical kit, ready to fix his arm. Orion cringed. He knew he needed to get it over with, but stitches, even with Pavo's quick light hand, were bound to be unpleasant.

"Hey, Castor." *Ugh.* He didn't like to even say it. "Dragon." *That's better.* "Go help Vela start the hovercraft. We've got to go get those meds. We nearly lost our nuts stealing that shipment. I'm not losing it."

"Got it."

There it was; that sweetness that made Orion's stomach flutter. He wanted to kiss it off of his adorable Dragon's face.

That boy is going to make the worst triad stooge. Not a drop of dishonor in him.

Orion could tell that's what Lynx was in training for. He knew the way around a weapon, and he had all those delicious muscles that Orion had felt under his fingers when they'd touched. He thought of that night again and smiled. He wanted more.

Orion needed to move. He could feel the blood shooting straight to his cock, and he knew there couldn't be a worse time for it.

"Pavo, let's get this over with. We have work to do." They needed to get rid of the shipment as soon as possible. Orion could never be caught with any of the stolen stuff anywhere near him.

Pavo was busily lining up bandages and skin adhesive. "I'm thinking we can get away without doing any stitching. Let me look at it."

Orion winced as Pavo unwrapped the fabric and pushed up his sleeve.

"Yeah," Pavo poked at the wound with a gloved hand. "Flesh wound, no bullet. We can use the adhesive. You'll be fine in a minute."

It felt like the longest minute he'd ever had to endure. Orion gritted his teeth as Pavo cleaned the wound then held the ragged edges together so he could apply the adhesive. After the liquid was in place, he ran a warm wand over the area, hardening the adhesive so that it held the wound together. Orion breathed a sigh of relief when Pavo wound a clean bandage around his arm.

"All done?"

"All done, boss. But, hey, take it easy. The rest of us can lift all of this stuff."

Orion nodded his thanks to Pavo and hopped off the storage container he'd been perched on. He bit his lip and smiled. He was actually having fun. It hadn't been fun in a really long time. Necessary, but not with the rush of exhilaration that was currently singing through him.

That's only because Dragon's here.

He'd even started thinking of Castor as Dragon. His Dragon. Annoying, argumentative, frustratingly elitist, but still the best time that Orion had had in ages.

With Dragon's help, Vela had pulled their ancient tank of a hovercraft around to the front of the building with Lynx's guidance. Orion motioned for Lynx to get on ahead of him and was a bit surprised when he didn't get a single objection. With Pavo and Seth in the seats behind them and the nimble Vela at the wheel, they whirred off into the thick, black underbrush toward the site where the meds had been dropped.

When they got there, everyone hopped off the craft,

ready to work, Orion included. The others tried to take his loads from him, but he wasn't wired that way. If his team worked, he worked too. Finally their craft was loaded and ready to go. Orion took a quick look at Pavo, Vela, and Seth.

"Dragon, start us up. You and I are going to take it. Guys, I'll message you the location. Meet us there in half an hour. Split up, and watch to make sure you're not followed. I don't want any of you to walk into a trap. If the triad goes after anyone, I want it to be me."

Orion glanced at Dragon, hoping that he wasn't offended that he'd been chosen to possibly walk into a trap. Pavo clearly was offended that he *hadn't* been chosen. Orion couldn't even say what his motivation was.

He could've said that he wanted to keep Kovalenko close, that he didn't quite trust him, and that was true...to a point. But Orion believed him when Lynx had said that he wasn't going to turn anyone in. It made no sense for them to be anything but enemies; they were from houses that were dead rivals, not that Dragon knew that, and everything he was doing stood against all that his flame-haired lover was, but Orion couldn't see him turning around and doing exactly what he'd already said he wouldn't do.

In a weird way, Orion did trust him.

And he wanted him near. He wanted to touch him and kiss him, wanted to be his lover again, like that very first night. He wanted to wrap his legs around his Dragon's waist and pull him into his body. He wanted to taste his kisses, wild and sweet, and kiss him in return, until they fell asleep naked and tangled, just like before.

Get a fucking grip, Orion Leonias. Shit.

THEY STARTED the hovercraft and made a sharp turn onto

one of the dilapidated streets of the ruin. The city must have been beautiful at one point, but the streets were cracked, and trees and blackened roots grew where there once were broad boulevards.

Orion would have loved to have seen the ruins before the war. He'd seen photographs, but it wasn't the same as being there.

It was too late, though. All that was left were a tumble of buildings, some partially habitable and some just piles of cement and wire, enshrouded by the stumpy blackened pines and cedars that grew, stunted by the lack of sun, turned black by the decades of polluted rain.

"Where are we going?" Dragon finally asked.

He'd waited in silence for long minutes, probably hoping that he was going to get some information.

"Somewhere I think you need to see," Orion finally answered.

"What do you mean?"

"You said you hated what we do. I want you to *see* what we really do. With your own eyes. I'm not so sure you'll hate it anymore."

"You give the medicine away — I already figured that out. I guess I see that you think you're doing a good thing. I don't understand, though. Bottom City people's bodies can't even handle them. They're born too deformed."

"Are you so sure about everything?"

"What are you not telling me?"

Orion gave the frustrated-looking Dragon a smile. Dragon huffed a little and sat back in his seat, hands loose on the steering wheel.

When they finally pulled up to the destination, the others were waiting for him. He'd had Dragon take a long windy path in case they had to lose somebody, but everything had seemed to be clear.

"'Took ya long enough" Pavo said with a smirk.

What did he think they were doing? Making out with the craft on idle? Orion colored. Was it written on his face how much he wanted Dragon? *Shit.* He needed to watch it when he was with his crew.

"Just wanted to make sure we didn't have any unwanted guests," he announced quietly and hopped out of the craft. "Let's get this baby unloaded, then I'm sending you guys home. After that stunt we pulled today, we're going to have to be extra careful for the next few days. I don't want to see any of you out here unless I send out an emergency message, and don't message me unless you've got one. I think it'll be best if we lay low until this blows over. It was close, and the triads are going to be pissed that we didn't get caught."

The others nodded, but Orion could tell they were disappointed. It had become their lives as well as his. None of them cared much about school, or triad business — other than what they could learn from spying on them. Everything they ever learned was passed back to him and used for the benefit of the Bottom City people.

"Yo, Dragon, help me with this box," called Pavo, always the first to listen to what Orion had to say. "Let's get the show going."

THEY WERE in front of an old warehouse; not too far from the city but outside any place that the triads would have patrols working. The warehouse looked like it was about to fall over. The wood was blackened with age and grime, and much of the glass had been shattered years before. Lynx shivered from the chill outside and the ice creeping up his back. The building had to be the spookiest, deadest-looking place he'd ever seen, even after his fairly extensive tours around the bombed-out ruins that day.

"What is this place?" he asked quietly.

Katana rolled his eyes and silently gestured for Lynx to follow. Lynx figured he should've known better than to actually *ask* for information. That, of course, would have been way too much.

He trusted Katana enough at that point to follow him without question, though. He doubted that after all of the shit they'd already been through that day that Katana would have some sort of mob waiting in the warehouse to take him down before he could tattle like the rich brat he probably seemed to be.

Inside the warehouse was absolute blackness, a combination of the perpetual night and a total lack of any artificial light. He stumbled and fell against Katana, who held him up with a strong arm.

"Sorry," he whispered, manners ingrained deeply in him coming to the surface.

Katana didn't answer but instead made a low haunting noise with his mouth that sounded to Lynx like one of the creatures they'd heard outside, a sound that he'd never encountered until that night. Katana made three long sounds, followed by a short noise, and two more long ones. The sequence was repeated and then Katana turned on a portable lamp. Other similar lights started flashing on all over the endless black space in the warehouse.

What Lynx saw make his eyes go wide. He held his breath then let it out long and slow, unable to even process what he was seeing. There were children, hundreds of them, some with parents, some on their own, wide-eyed and scared...and they were *perfect*.

He, along with everyone on the upper levels of the city, had been taught their entire lives that the bottom people were different, born deformed and unable to take the vitamins and medicines that everyone else took to combat the lack of light and the pollution.

They had been *lied* to.

The children in the room were normal sized, with hair that was thick and healthy. They were pale, yes, but none of them had those huge, lifeless black eyes. They simply looked like...like...well, like children.

Lynx watched, flabbergasted and silent, while the children lined up to get the medicine that they had stolen only hours before. He felt bad for the adults, fierce mothers only wanting to help their babies, parents so stunted and sickly that they probably wouldn't live to see their kids reach adulthood. But they were so grateful, giving toothless smiles to Katana as he doled out life-saving pills to their little ones.

"How did they know to come?" Lynx finally whispered, after most of the children had taken their dose and disappeared into the night.

"Pavo sends out encoded messages to the few who have the technology available to receive them. It's up to those people to spread the word, and they're more than willing to do so. These people help each other. It's so different from the backstabbing and petty shit that goes on up where we live."

Katana's face was soft, proud, and Lynx got it. He understood why it was so important, why Katana and his team had to keep going.

It wasn't a solution, it wasn't by any means perfect, but God, it was something. And it was all being done by the small, pale beauty who just that morning had been nothing but a mysterious lover who Lynx had wanted to find again. He reached out and touched a soft pink cheek, gratified when Katana trembled and rubbed his cheek against Lynx's palm.

He still wants me. Lynx smiled happily in the darkness. If anything, he cared more than he had that morning.

"C'mon," Katana whispered, when the last child had slipped into the darkness beyond their little pool of light. "Let's get back to the storage shed, and I'll show you the way back into the city."

THE SECOND THEY passed through the doorway into the storage shed, Orion slammed Dragon against the wall and covered Dragon's plump lips with his own hungry mouth. He hadn't meant to do it, hadn't planned it at all, but in that one second, it had all of a sudden become imperative.

All of the worry and adrenaline of the day had converged into one hot bolt of desire. The kiss was perfect. Delicious, lusty, and exactly what Orion had wanted since the night at the Phoenix bar. It felt like a millennia since he'd felt the thrill of Dragon's kiss.

Dragon moaned against his lips. "God, I've wanted you, I know I shouldn't, but I can't help it. Haven't stopped thinking of that night for days," he murmured.

Orion couldn't help but agree. "Me too. I've barely been able to concentrate on anything else. I think you're dangerous for me." It was true, but he said it with a smile.

Dragon smiled back and leaned forward for another kiss. Orion opened his mouth, wanting nothing more than the taste of Dragon's tongue sliding across his. He moaned quietly and pushed his fingers into that shock of soft bright hair, dragging him as close as possible. They kept at it, nibbling, licking, stealing hot kisses from each other's mouths, smiling when they drew away from each other.

"It's not too dangerous, though. We're safe here, right?"

"Safer than anywhere else," Orion answered and nipped at a full lower lip. "I want you inside me. Just like before."

His Dragon nodded, eyes wide, then started stripping Orion's clothes off. Weapons first, then overtunic, which was followed by wet kisses on his nipples, his collarbone, the line going from his belly down to the waist of his pants. Orion shivered and shimmied his hips, trying to say without words that he wanted more. Dragon looked up at him and smiled. Orion's boots came next, then his trousers were drawn down his legs until he was naked and waiting for Dragon's touch, just like the first perfect night.

"Yes," Orion murmured. "This is exactly what I want."

Dragon kissed his way back up Orion's legs, nuzzling him in the crease between his torso and his thighs. At the same time, his hands skimmed over Orion's chest, plucking at his sensitive, still-wet nipples.

"I wanted to do this so bad the last time," he murmured.

Wanted to do wha — ohhhh. Orion trembled and clutched at Dragon's shoulders, trying to grab on to something, anything, to keep his knees from buckling. He'd had it before, oral pleasure from the pretty mouths of socialites, both male and female, but it never felt anything like the spiraling bliss that was consuming him. Dragon sucked hard, making Orion's back arch. His skin broke out in goosebumps, and he shuddered.

"That's so *good.*"

And then Orion couldn't speak any more. He was shuddering toward a release he wasn't ready for. He wanted more. He wanted dragon inside of him, touching him, naked and chest to chest. Ah, God, it was going to be too late if he didn't —

"Stop," Orion moaned hoarsely. "C'mere. I want you now."

He tugged on Dragon's shoulders until he rose, licking and sucking his way back up his body. They touched and kissed, and Dragon pulled Orion's legs up to wrap around his waist, bringing them into full contact. Orion sucked a breath in.

"You have any lube in here?" Lynx asked, his breathing rough against Orion's neck.

Shit, Shit, Shit. "No. Of course not. Damn it." Orion was frustrated, but he couldn't help leaning over for another taste of skin. He sucked on his Dragon's neck, inhaling the newly familiar smell that drove him wild. "Still want you."

"It'll hurt you. I don't want to hurt you," Dragon muttered.

He was right. But it didn't stop Orion from want—*Ohh.* He felt the welcome pressure of fingers near his entrance. It was perfect.

"Don't care." Orion huffed out a harsh breath and keened, dropping his head back against the wall. "God, *yes.* In me."

"Yeah. We can...like this."

Dragon lifted his fingers to Orion's mouth, who took them in and slicked up the digits as much as he could. Then those same fingers were sinking into him, slow but persistent. Orion grappled with the hem of Dragon's tunic, drawing it up, getting frustrated by the snaps and ties of his complicated bottoms.

"I want to touch you," He whined, and Dragon fumbled with his free hand to get the annoying closures undone.

Orion had to slam his own hand against the wall to keep from falling. He was gripping Dragon's shoulder, head thrown back, feeling completely impaled by the fingers that were rubbing up against his prostate. How did his Dragon know exactly how to touch him? Orion didn't care. However he knew what to do, it was perfect.

Orion sighed when he finally got a hold on Dragon's cock, hard and dripping with excitement. He'd wanted to touch it for days. Dragon slammed their lips together in another desperate kiss, tongue plunging into Orion's more than willing mouth.

They stayed that way for long minutes, wanting more but feeling too good to stop. Orion could barely breathe, couldn't talk, think, anything but *feel*. That was the only thing his brain had room to do.

He groaned and clutched at Dragon's shoulder with his free hand. Dragon backed them all the way against the wall and held him pinned there, so close, Orion could feel every rise and fall of Dragon's labored breathing. The kisses just got wetter and hotter, both of them licking and biting and using the other's hair to pull closer, closer. There was no such thing as close enough. Orion's head spun from lack of air. He could care less. He never wanted any of it to end.

"So sexy," Dragon murmured when they pulled apart, gasping for breath. Then he bent his head to suck on Orion's neck.

It was too much — the built-up desire, the touches and those kisses that made his heart feel like it was going to beat right out of his chest. He was spiraling out of control so fast, and he could see little black stars at the edge of his vision bursting in time with his galloping pulse.

"Can't wait anymore," he gasped.

"Yes, come. Wanna feel it all over me."

The words pushed him over the edge. Orion ground his face into Dragon's neck and let everything go. He came, shouting, riding Dragon's fingers and holding on to that slick cock like it just might save his life. A few strokes with his trembling hand, and Dragon was following, shooting warmth onto Orion's exposed stomach.

It took a few minutes for the spinning to stop, for their breath to calm down, their hearts to stop trying to punch through their skin so they could touch, free in the cool air of the storage shed. Orion was barely conscious. His eyes were closed, and he couldn't imagine conjuring the energy to open them. He just stayed there, limp and wrapped around Dragon's body.

"Holy shit," Dragon murmured, his voice hoarse.

"No kidding. Wasn't expecting *that*." Orion felt the soft chuckle against his chest.

"Me neither. How could I? Never felt anything like it."

Lynx backed away slowly, his arms still looped loosely around him, and let him slide down the wall until his feet were back on solid ground. They stood there trembling for long seconds before Dragon slowly and gently pulled his fingers from the tightness of his body. Orion felt a moment of loss but was distracted when Dragon slipped his other hand underneath the heavy fall of his hair and lifted it from his sweaty neck, blowing on the skin beneath.

"Mmm, that's nice." Orion couldn't help the contented purring sound that came from his throat.

"So you wanna get back to the city?"

Orion groaned softly. "Not really."

Lynx pulled off his tunic and offered Orion his undershirt to clean up. "You've got to go back too, don't you?"

"Yeah." Orion peeled himself from the wall and wiped

off before reluctantly starting to pull his clothes back on. "But I'd rather stay."

Dragon gave him a soft smile. "Me too. I want to stay with you. I mean, I want to come back. I want to help. I... understand now. I had no idea."

Orion traced his thumb along Dragon's cheekbone. "You weren't supposed to know. No one is. Can you imagine what would happen if the people found out that generations of children are allowed to grow, deformed and sick, because of basic lack of health care that we can easily get them?"

Dragon shrugged. "Do you think anyone would care?"

"Do you?"

"Of course."

"Then I can only hope others would too."

They were both silent for a long time. "I don't understand why they stay," Dragon finally said. "For us, I get it. It's nice where we live. But for them?"

They paid the price for decades of darkness. A price people in Cloud City tried to brush under the proverbial rug.

Orion shook his head. "Where do you think they're going to go, Dragon? Nobody else wants them."

"Uh, um...Katana?" he hesitated, stumbling on the name.

Orion made a quick decision. "Call me Rion. Nobody calls me Katana. It's just a hacker alias."

"Ryan?" He looked surprised. "You're about twenty, right?" Orion nodded. "How'd you happen to get out of one of the space cadet star names like mine?"

Back around the time of their birth, it had been a trend for highborn children to be named after the stars that barely anyone alive had seen — and Orion *had* been stuck with one of the star names. It could've been worse. One of his cousins got slapped with Camelopardalis. He regularly threatened to throttle people who called him anything but Cam.

Orion shrugged, not correcting Dragon. There were quite a few Orions in New Seattle, but it was easiest to leave it the way it was.

"Guess I got lucky. Parents didn't want to torture me like everyone else. Does your family call you something else? Castor doesn't seem to fit you."

Dragon shook his head. Orion thought that he might look a bit embarrassed. That cemented it. His Dragon *wasn't* Castor Kovalenko. That much was clear. Although Orion didn't know who Dragon was, he vowed to find out soon enough.

"Well, I'm calling you Dragon. The other one doesn't work for me."

"That's fine." Dragon smiled at him.

Orion sighed reluctantly. "Hey, we'd better get going. As much as I'd rather stay out here forever, I gotta get topside tonight. It's family dinner."

He made a very genuine gagging sound. He hated sitting at the family table on Sunday nights, pretending to care about whatever Aries was ranting about, or about the decorations for his mothers' latest party. Sometimes dinner produced some good intel. Usually it was just a headache.

"I've gotta get back too. I was going to ask you how. I've been gone for way too long. Don't want to go, though."

He trailed his fingers up the inside of Orion's leg and reached into his still loose trousers and cupped his softening flesh. He smiled then, and leaned over to brush Orion's swollen lips with one more soft kiss.

Chapter Seven

LYNX STRUGGLED to look alert as he made his way to the dining area of Dragon house. He had a splitting headache from lack of sleep and the weirdest feeling that if he didn't get out of his family's opulent prison very soon, he was going to burst into a million pieces.

More than anything, he wanted to be back in the ruins with Ryan — not the stealthy and ingenious Katana, but Ryan the pale beauty, who made his heart and skin and everything in between tingle with newfound life. He'd never realized how much he was suffocating until he'd had a taste of the way it could be.

He grabbed a carafe of coffee, thinking he'd probably need to drink the entire thing before he felt like a human again, and collapsed into one of the plush dining room chairs. Much of the previous night had been spent lying awake, wishing he could feel Ryan's body next to his, naked and smooth and slick with perspiration.

Lynx wondered how he could have gotten to such a dire state of infatuation after just one hot night and that crazy, crazy day they'd spent together. There was no need to examine it, though. The truth was in the melting feeling he had in his belly every time he thought of Ryan's throaty laugh. Lynx knew it — he was so unbelievably gone.

"Hey, Cousin!"

"Morning!"

Shit. Lynx had been hoping to avoid them. He didn't want to have to answer too many questions. Misdirection time.

"Check out the new sausage, guys. It's pretty good. You can hardly taste the soy paste."

Most meat products were in fact comprised of soy proteins that were harvested in labs down in Metrolevel. Only the rare person had tasted anything different, but the lesser quality 'meats' still had a funny aftertaste. Castor snagged a link from Lynx's plate and took a casual bite from it.

"Eh, not bad." Then he winked at Lynx. "Good try, cuz, but it's not going to work. Where were you yesterday? Marco was looking for you when you missed Jujitsu."

Lynx tried to hide his blush, but it was impossible. He hated that quality of his.

"It's the same place you disappeared to last time, isn't it? You've got a new piece. What's her name?"

He blushed, if anything, even harder. "What are you talking about? There's no girl."

Castor and Pollux traded conspiratorial glances.

"Fine, then. It's not a *girl*, but there is someone, isn't there?" Pollux's grin grew. "That's cool, cuz. Cas and I have both had our share of pretty boys coming and going. You know there's no shame there."

Lynx hated to think of Ryan as the no-strings piece of ass his cousin was implying. He was *so* much more.

"That's not it."

"Yeah, it is, and it's great that you're not thinking about Celes — aw, shit, you're doing it again, aren't you? That thing where you jump into a relationship with both of your balls. You just broke up with someone. Haven't you ever heard of playing the field? Getting as much as you can from wherever you can get it?"

The thought of touching anyone other than Ryan made Lynx want to puke. He was in that deep. "*Shit*, guys. Can I please just have some coffee in peace? I'm perfectly capable of running my own love life, thanks."

"See, he called it his *looooove* life." Castor and Pollux poked at each other and chuckled.

"That's not what I— Just go do whatever it is you two were planning to do and leave me alone. I slept like shit last night."

"We were actually coming to find you and tell you that the governor has called an official meeting for tonight. All upper Dragon and Phoenix triad members are required to attend."

"What for? She want us to promise to play nice again? It's never going to happen, no matter how many arms laws she passes."

"No. I actually think it's about Yoru Katana. He nabbed another huge shipment yesterday. They nearly caught him, but he slipped away. This time, the Dragons and the Phoenixes have to work together. He's all of our problems."

Lynx smiled at the memory of his adventure the previous day, an odd-looking reaction, he was sure, but he couldn't bring himself to care.

Ryan...

He doubted that any meeting with the Phoenix triad would worry Ryan. The triads didn't know a thing about his operation. Talking wouldn't make a damn bit of difference.

But maybe he could find time to slip away and warn him anyway. He did need to know, right? Lynx's smile broadened.

"What the hell's your problem, cuz? Why you smiling about Katana?"

"Or working with the fucking Phoenixes? I'd rather kill them."

Lynx caught himself and schooled his face to look more sober. "I'm not. I'm just tired, that's all. I'll be at the meeting. Don't worry."

"I know you will. Pol and I will be at your room at six. Be ready."

"What? You're policing me?"

"You've been a little weird lately."

Yeah. Weird. Turned upside down and had all his loose change shaken out was more like it. Lynx didn't know how to act like the same person he'd been before he met Ryan. He didn't know if that person existed any longer. It wasn't just about falling for Ryan's sexy laugh and gorgeous face, either. It was about Katana, and how what he was doing was *right*, no matter how illegal it was.

Lynx already had plans to meet him the next morning to detail another operation. He was all in, just like his cousins had said, playing with his life and his heart. He didn't think there was any other way.

LYNX HAD MANAGED to fall asleep for a while but was awoken by the sibilant hiss of his chamber door sliding open.

"You're not ready? Hurry, Lynx. Your father will fry us alive if we're not there on time."

Lynx bolted out of bed, the surprise of Pollux's loud voice jolting him to life. "Sorry guys. I guess I really was tired. Give me two minutes, and I'll be ready to go."

After a scrambled attempt at dressing and taming his flaming sunset-colored spikes of hair, he followed his cousins out the door and to the lift that would take them to the Metrolevel government complex where the meeting was going to be taking place.

"Tell us more about this dude you've been boning, cousin."

Lynx groaned. "I never said there was a guy. You two decided there was."

"Give it up, Lynx. You're easier to read than anyone I've ever met. There's a boy."

They'd gotten off the lift and were on the sky bridge that led to one of the public meeting rooms in the middle of the ineffectual government's midcity compound. The meeting had to be held somewhere that was far from either Phoenix or Dragon home territory, and while the government had little real power out in the city, at least neither triad had infiltrated their buildings.

Lynx sighed as they passed through the weapon detector and surrendered their fingers for the customary body-enhancing drug and subdermal weapons test.

"Drop it, Cas. I'm not telling you two anything. The last thing I need is to have my personal life broadcasted all over Cloud Level. You guys are worse than a couple of teenage girls."

"Fine," Castor huffed and shuffled through the portal into the meeting room.

Lynx and his two cousins took their seats among the Dragon nobility. His cousins immediately started watching the main door and making comments about the Phoenix leaders who were filing in.

Lynx had never paid much attention to the Leonias family before — or the Phoenix triad, for that matter. He'd spent his youth reading old books set in long-ago places, where the people didn't get along much better than they did now but at least had fewer vices available to them and far fewer stretches of useless free time. He envied those long-gone people.

Lynx found himself thinking of Ryan again as he half listened to his cousins gossip. He wondered what Ryan was doing, if he was out with friends, or if he, like Lynx, preferred to stay at home and read. He wondered if Ryan was...

"Oh, that's Cassiopeia Leonias, the daughter. Pretty. Heard she's locked up like a nun, though."

Pollux chuckled. "Not like the son. He's always at all the right parties. At least the ones that a Dragon can't get into."

"Ooh, there he is. That's Orion," Castor hissed. "Damn. I'd love to let him sit on my lap for an hour or two. He's even prettier than the girl."

"He's a Phoenix, Cas. You're such a fucking horn-o"

"So? Look at his *ass*. Perfection like that can cross triad lines."

Pollux chuckled, and Lynx lifted his head, mildly curious about the specimen of male beauty that was Orion Leonias. From the back he was lithe and graceful, and Lynx had to admit the guy's hair was pretty, a long sparkling tail of deep blue that somehow seemed to glow. He had his head turned, and all Lynx could see was his light step and — *oh my god*. Orion Leonias lifted his head to look right at their table. His gaze connected with a very shocked Lynx. *Ryan?* It all started to make horrible sense.

Ryan's, or rather *Orion's* eyes, widened for a brief moment before he flashed Lynx a beseeching smile and sat at his parents' table. Lynx was reeling. His Ryan, his Katana, was *Orion Leonias*, first and only son of the Phoenix triad? He all of a sudden felt like he was going to vomit. Lynx dropped his head toward his knees and tried to concentrate on breathing.

It was then that he realized the other part of the problem, and if anything, his nausea increased.

It wasn't going to take Rion more than one good long look to figure out that he wasn't Castor Kovalenko. The twins were sitting right next to him, obviously identical, and he was clearly not one of them.

He's gonna know I lied.

Lynx wanted to moan out loud. He saw the moment that Orion realized what he was seeing. He rose from his chair and started to make his way across the still noisy room toward the table where Lynx and his cousins were sitting — cowering was more like it. Lynx wished fervently that he could sink into the ground.

When Orion got to their table, he sank into one of the empty chairs, close enough that Lynx could smell that same intoxicating sweetness that had driven him wild the day before. His smile was serene and cool, nothing like the lively grin Lynx had seen in the ruins. Lynx hated it.

"I'm Orion Leonias. I figured since our families were here with white flags flying, I ought to come and be social."

Castor laughed. "Well, you've just got cousins and a middle son here. You should probably go make nice with Leo over there. He's the oldest son, heir to the triad, like you."

"Two cousins and a mere middle son?" Orion made a fake scornful face and everyone chuckled nervously. "I take it you two are Castor and Pollux, which would make you..."

Orion turned that weird serene glance over to Lynx. It made him squirm in his seat, because he could feel the irritation that was underneath that unrippled surface. He couldn't believe his cousins were immune to it.

"This is Lynx."

"Ah. Lynx Kovalenko. You don't say." Rion smiled and rose from his seat. "Well, it was pleasant to meet you three. I'd better retreat back to my side of the battlefield."

"Sit with us. They're starting anyway. I don't bite, promise — not in a bad way at least."Castor said, flipping a flirtatious smile in Rion's direction.

Lynx wanted to take a chunk out of his cousin's throat.

The meeting was indeed starting, both Phoenix and Dragon leaders shuffling to their seats and quieting. Orion shrugged and remained seated right next to Lynx, whose own body was emanating tense irritation, he was sure.

"How do you find the meeting so far *Lynx*?" Orion muttered.

"It's not like you told me who you were either," Lynx whispered back. He was having a hard time keeping his voice to near silent level.

"I didn't lie to your face and give you the wrong name."

"Oh, really, *Ryan*?"

"That's the *truth*. My family calls me that, Pavo and the others too. Didn't you know I'd eventually figure out you weren't one of the twins?"

Lynx turned to face Rion but sat slowly back in his seat when he noticed Castor and Pollux's curious stares.

"I didn't foresee this little scenario for sure. I do like your hair though. Pretty."

Lynx tried to make it sound as insulting as possible. He must have hit a nerve. Orion flipped his hair over his shoulder and turned to glare at Lynx. Those same big eyes that had once been filled with lust and admiration were angry, annoyed. Lynx regretted his little petty jab immediately. All he wanted was for Orion to smile at him again.

"Rion,"

Orion rolled his eyes and looked over. "What do you want?"

"I'm sorry. I wanted to tell you who I was after I realized that I trusted you. I just didn't know how to tell you that I 'd lied in the first place."

"It doesn't matter."

"Yes, it *does*."

"Shhhh. Just listen."

The governor had been droning on and on about the growing troubles with the theft of medicine, and how it was taking away valuable medicine from the people of New Seattle.

What a bunch of crap. The companies that the triads ran could easily manufacture more of the product. They just didn't want to lose out on the revenue — nor did they want to provide it at a reasonable price to the Bottom City poor. Even Lynx knew that much. And he *cared*. Things that would have meant nothing to him days before made his hackles rise up.

"I still want to help you," he murmured, making sure that his voice didn't carry past Rion's ear.

"Dragon, be quiet. We'll talk later."

Lynx nodded.

"... so Phoenix and Dragon leaders, what can we do together to stop this theft from escalating?" The governor, who Lynx had been ignoring, finally wrapped up her speech.

"Katana is a Dragon."

A voice boomed from the middle of the Phoenix side of the room. Both Lynx and Rion froze, suddenly alert, their whispered argument forgotten for the moment.

"What grounds do you have for such an accusation?" The governor looked sincerely perplexed.

Lynx's father on the other hand looked about ready to explode. "No Dragon would steal from his own family. What kind of lie is this?"

Aries Leonias stood. *Shit.* Lynx had a sinking feeling in his gut.

"One of the thieves, and we believe it to be Katana, since he stayed behind and covered the others, had the sunburst red hair that only a Kovalenko would have."

"That can be done in any salon."

"It didn't look dyed, Kovalenko. He was a Dragon."

"So the thief went to a *good* salon. That only means he has plenty of stolen money, not that he is a relative of mine." Yuri Kovalenko's voice was dripping with condescension meant to get right under Aries' skin.

"*Gentlemen.*"

Lynx's heart was pounding. He was sure that every person in the room was staring at him. It was only going to be a matter of seconds before Aries spotted him. *Oh, God.* He felt a hand on his knee, soft and reassuring.

"There's no way he saw your face," Rion whispered, a thread of sound right against Lynx's ear. And he was right, Lynx hoped. He didn't know what would happen to him if he were identified.

The argument over the mysterious flame-haired thief

went on for long horrible minutes. Lynx was sure that at any moment, Aries would point his way.

A small, panicky bit of Lynx wanted to turn himself in to end the torture. There was one good thing to come out of his momentary ordeal. Orion had immediately gone from annoyed and distrustful to supportive, the hand on his knee sending silent strength.

"It's fine, Dragon," he finally whispered and slid his hand slowly from Lynx's knee. Lynx felt the loss but remained silent, waiting for the topic of the mysterious Dragon to die.

THE MEETING ENDED at a tense impasse, the Phoenix lords shooting angry glares toward the Dragon half of the room, the Dragons full of righteous indignation. Lynx didn't have a good feeling about the outcome of the night. It was likely that what was arguing in front of the law enforcement that ringed the conference room would turn into outright warfare as soon as the two triads were no longer being actively policed.

However uneasy things were, though, the Dragon and Phoenix triads did decide to band together publicly against the outlaw Katana, and both volunteered guard forces to patrol the shipping docks.

Great, our job just got that much harder.

Even with the revelation of Rion's true identity, Lynx hadn't for a second thought about not working with him again. They'd been equal in their distrust, and both had withheld information about their names. Lynx cared, a little, but not enough to stay away from Orion or the cause he already cared about.

He tried to catch Orion's attention in the shuffling that

always ended a public meeting. The shuffling that night was paired with animosity between the triads, even with their agreement to work together. Lynx hated the uncomfortable half peace and the uneasiness he felt every time he looked at Orion's chill serenity. Where was the spitfire he knew? Lynx barely recognized his passionate lover under the socialite's perfect mask.

Lynx put his hand on Orion's wrist, barely caring if his cousins saw.

"Tomorrow?" He whispered, before it was too late and his lover had slipped away. He needed to be sure of them again. His chest hurt with every beat of uncertainty.

Orion's face twisted in regret, something real finally showing through. "Dragon, we can't. It's too much, you being the son of Kovalenko, and me being, well, *me*."

"We're the same people we always were. I'm coming tomorrow." Lynx pursed his lips, hoping that his resolve showed.

Orion shook his head. "I won't be there. Forget about me, Dragon. It was a bad idea from the start."

He slipped away then, leaving Lynx looking after him wistfully. Lynx wasn't going to give up. Not a fucking chance. He'd go to the hideout in the ruins the next day and talk some sense into Rion.

They could help each other, they needed each other.

Lynx had never wanted anyone so much in his life. Before he met Rion, he hadn't thought it was possible to *feel* so strongly.

He resolved it right then. *Tomorrow. No matter where I have to go, I'm going to talk to him tomorrow.*

LYNX CREPT through the deserted indoor boulevards of Cloud Level toward the heavily guarded Leonias estate. He'd spent the day searching the ruins for signs of Rion, but he'd found nothing except for a deserted old storage unit.

It stung that Rion felt like he had to move his operation because Lynx knew where it was located. Was he suddenly untrustworthy because of his name? He wished he *were* Castor. Perhaps then he'd be with Rion, instead of slinking through a neighborhood where his very name made him a target.

He said a few silent prayers before he stepped up to the gate. He tucked a dyed strand of hair behind his ear, trying to tame the habitual spikes. He'd dressed in typical servant garb, pilfered from his house: black slacks, shoes, and a long black button-down shirt. The fabric was itchy to skin accustomed to the finest of materials. He didn't care. Any amount of discomfort was worth it if he were successful.

"Purpose?" Barked a voice through the callbox.

"Night duty. I'm filling in for Mel O'Toole."

Lynx had done his homework. He knew that one of the Phoenix servants was sick. He also knew they'd be looking for the temporary replacement that had been ordered — the one who was currently taking a nice long tranquilizer-induced nap in one of the Kovalenko family's hovercrafts.

"You're fifteen minutes late. Get to the house immediately."

Lynx slipped through the gate, head down so the guard didn't see the clarity of his skin or his expensive haircut. Night-shift servants tended to be from lower Midtown, poorly nourished and barely educated, a few slim levels from being the pariahs of Bottom City.

They did the jobs that no one wanted to see during the day — floor scrubbing, toilet cleaning, everything that the day servants would refuse to do and machinery could never get quite right. He wanted to slip into the house, but he had to be careful not to get noticed. It was to his advantage that no one seemed to look past a servant's black garb.

"Get to the kitchens, boy. They'll have a list of duties for you there."

Lynx nodded and scurried toward the servants' entrance, trying his best to look meek. As soon as he got inside, he withdrew from the front of his shirt the small sketch of the estate that he'd made. He had to make it unseen through the main sections of the house and into Orion's bedroom.

Lynx grabbed some kind of cleaning tool; he hoped he wouldn't have to use it, because he had no idea what it was for other than cover. With tool in hand, he headed for the area of the house where he knew Orion's room was located.

It had taken some effort, getting the plans for the Leonias house, but he was good with computers. Perhaps he wasn't quite as nimble as Yoru Katana, but good enough to perform some routine hacking. After that, it hadn't taken too much detective work to figure out which entrance code belonged to Orion's personal butler, and then it was fairly obvious which suite of rooms were Orion's. Now he just had to get to them without being killed, use the code that he'd memorized, and hope that Rion was willing to listen to him.

LYNX BREATHED a sigh of relief when he was standing outside of what he was nearly sure were Orion's rooms. He'd be in a whole hell of a lot of trouble if he was wrong, but it was a chance he had to take. He tapped the entrance code that belonged to Rion's manservant into the key box outside the door and held his breath as the door slid sound-lessly open.

The room was clean, luxurious, but lacking in the opulence that the rest of the house was draped in. Lynx closed the door and crept as silently as possible across glossy bamboo flooring toward the low, soft bed that he saw crouched in a far corner.

When he got there, he froze, unable to decide what his next step should be. Orion was sleeping, his face calm, the brilliant mass of his hair spilling over the pillow. It really was beautiful. Lynx's fingers had itched to touch it when it was dyed black, but the pure shining blue was nearly irre-sistible. Lynx wanted to bury his fists in it and pull Rion closer, he wanted to —

"Get out, or I'll call security." Orion's voice was quiet but strong, his real voice, not the cultured tone of Orion the socialite.

"It's me. Lynx. I have to talk to you." Lynx's heart pounded nervously. *Please hear me out.*

"Lynx?...*Dragon.*" Orion stood quickly and moved toward Lynx, shooing him to the door. "You can't be here." He spoke quietly, but with force. "Are you trying to start a war?"

"I went to the ruins, but you weren't there. I can't believe you don't trust me — Listen, I just need to talk to you."

"What is there to say?" Orion looked a bit sad but resolute.

"There's *everything* to say," Lynx whispered, as force-fully as he could. "How 'bout I still want to be a part of what you're doing? How about I don't want to — no, I *can't stand* to walk away and never see you again."

"Dragon, we can't, our families."

Rion had drifted closer, his hand grazing Lynx's chest. Lynx felt his pulse pounding. All he wanted in the world was to be able to kiss Orion again.

"You knew I was a Dragon before. It didn't seem to bother you so much two days ago."

"But that was when you were Castor, unimportant cousin, not Lynx, son of Yuri Kovalenko."

Lynx's eyes narrowed. "You never thought I was Castor. You know enough about my cousins that there was no way you'd mistake me for one of them."

Orion sighed, then dipped his chin in a slight nod. "You're right. I didn't think you were Castor. It seemed all wrong. But I didn't know who you were, and that's the truth." He lifted his hand to cup Lynx's chin. "I wish we weren't so impossible, Dragon. For that one day…" He laughed mirthlessly. "I wanted us as much as you did me."

"But it's not impossible. I want to be with you. You make me feel *real* when nothing else ever did."

"Lynx, no."

It was the first time Orion had called him by his real name, other than that scornful whisper back at the meeting. It made Lynx's heart trip in his chest.

"Yes. *Please.* That night, and then out in the ruins. I can't give that up, Rion. I can't give *you* up."

"You have to. It's too dangerous for us to know each other, and I refuse to compromise my cover. Not for anything."

"Not even this?"

Lynx dove in and covered Orion's lips with his own, sinking his fingers into the warm blue fall of silk and angling Orion's head so that his lips were open for the plunder.

Orion didn't fight but instead wrapped his arms around Lynx's shoulders and met Lynx's tongue with his own, moaning and gasping and rolling his hips. The kiss was desperate, punishing, Orion biting at Lynx's lips, Lynx pulling hard on Orion's hair. Lynx felt it hit him, anger and glory thrumming through his body.

They were so *right* together. How could Orion let it go? He bit harder, the new taste of blood flavoring the kiss. Orion groaned and pulled at him, grinding his hips into Lynx's — pleasure to the point of pain.

When they broke apart, they were panting, lips swollen and bruised, skin flushed, eyes glassy with need. As much as he hated it, Lynx saw the ending in Orion's face. He knew that no matter how much they wanted to be near each other, Orion would never choose Lynx over his cause. Orion finally spoke, his voice steady, only his face betraying the fact that it was actually hard for him to say the words.

"Good-bye, Lynx Kovalenko. As much as I want you, I *can* give you up. I have to." He closed his eyes and ran his fingers over Lynx's cheek one more time. "I'm going to give you fifteen minutes to get out of here, then I'm calling security. I suggest you move quickly."

Lynx saw a momentary flash of pain, but it was covered up quickly. He knew that Orion would do exactly as he said. Lynx turned and walked, his heart burning, toward the door.

"Dragon?" Orion called softly.

Lynx turned and froze, hoping against unrealistic hope that Orion had changed his mind.

"Don't come looking for me. I don't want to be found, and the ruins aren't a safe place for you if you're alone."

Lynx gave a stiff nod and turned, trying to swallow around the huge lump in his throat.

Chapter Eight

ORION'S CHEST HURT. It had for more than a week, and he didn't know what to do to fix it. He tried telling himself that Lynx was just a fling. He'd had his share of flings hot and not so hot, and just because the sex had been mind-meltingly amazing, it shouldn't have made the whole thing a big deal.

He tried repeating his own words, the ones he'd said to Lynx. *It's impossible, our families are enemies, it's too dangerous.* While he believed what he said, it didn't help the fluttery ache that never seemed to go away unless he thought of Lynx and how amazing it felt to hold him.

"Boss, what's your problem? Did you get the specs for the new shipping tunnel?"

The Phoenix triad had started work on a new shipping facility, one that went underground and would be guarded so heavily, it would be nearly impossible for Orion and his crew to get in.

He'd been trying to get into the system and download the specs, which would usually be no problem for him to get, but he'd been so distracted lately, that it simply hadn't happened. He needed those specs, though. He needed to get his head out of his ass was more like it. Sitting around and moping over Dragon wasn't going to do anyone any good, and if he was stupid enough over it, it could end up getting him killed.

"Rion, seriously, what's up with you lately? You've been all weird since last week. *Oh*, I get it. It's Kovalenko, huh?" Pavo was looking at him with a raised eyebrow.

Orion winced but didn't reply.

"What's up with that? You're never like this over some guy."

"He's not —" Orion caught himself before he finished the sentence. Lynx *wasn't* just some guy, though. Not even that first night. He was different.

God, I'm an idiot.

Orion wished he could smack some sense into himself. He had plans, and none of them included falling in love. Again he winced. He couldn't believe he'd used those words, even in his head. *Get a grip. You've got work to do.*

"I'll get the specs ready, so we can work on a plan tomorrow. I've got to make an appearance at a few butterfly parties this weekend."

He rolled his eyes, not only to make Pavo laugh, but also in the hope that his moping over Lynx would be forgotten. Pavo thankfully got the hint and left him alone to his thoughts.

In his distracted state, it took Orion way too long to hack into the city's database of approved plans and specs. He was lucky that the triad had to play it by the rules and submit plans for the new tunnel.

If the project had been smaller, they might have flown it

under the government radar. If they'd done that, he would have been screwed, or at least had to do some much more involved snooping. The specs for the new tunnel were housed on the city Web site, along with the plans for his family's estate on Cloud Level and their original shipping docks. He began downloading all the specs into their system but got annoyed when it moved too slow. The file was huge, and his computers were not the newest machinery.

To pass time, and perhaps out of a bit of curiosity, Orion pulled up the plans for his family's house. He flipped through them, identifying his rooms, the kitchen, the main area where his family entertained. He'd spent a lot of time learning the tunnels and back ways in and out of the shipping ports of Bottom City from reading plans just like this and was nearly as proficient at it as the architects who'd rendered them in the first place.

Orion noticed that the tunnel specs were done loading and had moved his hand to the right of the screen to close down the house plans when he noticed something that seemed a bit off.

Near the back service entry to the offices on the third floor, there was another room depicted on the plans. It would be small, perhaps perfect for a large bathroom or a small office, but no matter how many ways Orion oriented the plans on his screen, he couldn't force them to make sense. That room wasn't there. It would be behind a large holoscreen that was mounted on the wall in the conference room, and well, it just wasn't there, simple as that. It couldn't be.

"Hey, Pav, come check this out," Orion called out.

Pavo stuck his head around the corner from the room next door, looking excited. "Got the specs, boss?"

"Well, yeah, but that's not what I want you to look at. C'mere."

Pavo came into the room and leaned over Orion's deck, looking perplexed. "Isn't that just a house?"

"Yeah," Orion grunted. "It's mine. But see this room here?" Orion pointed on the plans, and Pavo nodded. "It isn't there."

"What do you mean?"

"I mean, that room is on the papers, but it's not in my house."

"Well, maybe the builder changed their plans."

"Not without registering new ones. And look, these walls are all the same, and that wall is an exterior wall. It can't be changed."

"What, so you think that room is there but hidden?"

"It seems to be the logical explanation, but that's ridiculous, isn't it? Why would my dad need a secret room in his own offices?"

Pavo gave Orion a long sympathetic look. Orion sighed. "Okay, he could probably be doing a lot of things back there. *Fuck*. We don't need something else to deal with."

"Then don't deal with it. Maybe it's just your dad's kinky porn collection or something, and he doesn't want anyone to know. Ooooh, maybe he has, like, a little minidungeon in there, and him and your mom get all freaky."

Orion chuckled and shoved at Pavo.

"Gross. Seriously, though. I wish I could just dismiss it. But I'm gonna have to check it out. Otherwise, it's gonna drive me nuts. Just have to get my father to leave that office he practically lives in."

"Isn't there a party this weekend? Slip away and do some snooping."

Orion nodded. "At least it's my own damn house, and if I get caught, I can play drunk and dumb."

Pavo shook his head. "I still don't know how they believe it. Your brains are right there in your eyes, so easy to see."

Orion shrugged. "I make it easy for them to believe and it's what they want to see, so I don't have much trouble convincing anyone."

"Why don't I look over the specs for the tunnel, and you go get ready for your parents' party? Tell me later what you find."

Orion nodded, looking forward to getting back to his family's house for the first time in a really long time.

ORION FELT VAGUELY uncomfortable in his expensive society clothes, which was a little weird, since he'd been wearing some version of the same thing every weekend for years. Each time he put on one of his diaphanous androgynous outfits and lined his eyes with shimmering colored powders, it felt less and less like him.

Even his own hair, which he preferred to the necessary black, seemed like it should belong to someone else. Orion looked in the mirror and sighed at the pale delicate flower that he saw there. It *wasn't* him anymore — probably never had been.

The real him was squirming inside that serene shell, dying to get on with his mission instead of socializing and pretending to drink the strong punch, which was usually spiked with pleasure-inducing drugs that kept the parties at a high fervor.

Mingle, wait till everyone's drunk or high on whatever they took, then disappear.

He had no idea how he was going to stand waiting that long. He shrugged. Didn't have much of a choice.

THE PARTY WAS JUST LIKE every other party, filled with colorful expensive clothes, elaborate hair, voracious drinking, and copious drug use. It used to be a thrill to attend the parties, get sucked into the whirling colorful dervish of drugs and sex. But that was back when he was younger and dying to be let free from the safe cloisters of his family's estate.

Lately, if it hadn't been necessary to perpetuate his cover, Orion wouldn't have had anything to do with them. All he saw were people enjoying excesses that were paid for by the blood and sweat of Bottom City.

His friends greeted him, flitting by with drinks in hand and half-aware smiles hovering on their lips. Orion smiled back and raised his own glass. Eventually, even the half-awareness was gone, and all that was left were numbed-out revelers who would never notice his absence. Orion walked slowly, so as not to call attention to himself, toward the business wing of his family's estate.

Fairly soon, he was far from the music and clinking glasses, walking along the more serviceable hallways of the office area. He was about to turn into the conference room, where he planned to start his search, when he was startled by a figure at the end of the hall. Even with hair dyed a warm brown and contacts covering those incredible grass-green eyes, Orion knew who it was immediately. He tried to control the happy little jump that his insides performed.

"You're insane, aren't you?" He hissed, only lowering his voice slightly in the deserted hallway.

"I feel like I am. I've tried, Rion. For *days*. It's not getting any better."

"*Lynx*." He went to slip away but stopped when Lynx grabbed his arm.

"No."

He looked serious and more intimidating that Orion had ever seen him.

"You're not saying no again. You want this just as much as I do."

Lynx crowded Orion into the wall with his muscular body. His face looked possessive, angry. Orion breathed in, surprised there were little flutters warming his stomach.

What happened to his sweet Dragon? He tried half-heartedly to push Lynx off but couldn't. Lynx wouldn't budge. He had his arm across Orion's chest, blocking any possible movement. His lips went to Orion's neck, and he sucked hard, making violent chills rock Orion's body.

"Lynx, stop. We can't."

"You want this. I know you do."

He did. *Oh*, he did. More than anything he could ever remember wanting before. He groaned when Lynx's hand slipped between them to cup his rapidly hardening cock.

"I want you to *go*." It was nearly impossible for Orion to spit out the lie. His voice wasn't convincing. Even he could tell. "I'm going to call security."

"No, you're not."

Lynx gentled his touch. Possession became caressing, his tongue trailing up the side of Orion's neck in a barely-there caress. He slid a thigh between Orion's legs and ground them together.

"You want me here, in your bed, in your body. You want to feel us together again."

Orion moaned and gripped Lynx's neck. He felt like he was drowning. He knew what they were doing was suicidal, but it was getting harder and harder to care.

"Lynx, I—"

"*Shhhh.*"

Orion froze. Then he heard it too, footsteps coming down the hall, about to turn the corner. *Shit.*

"*Kiss* me," He whispered, then grabbed Lynx by the neck and dragged him in.

A little love in the dark hallway was the best excuse he could think of for being away from the party. The best excuse he could think of to kiss Lynx too. And he wanted to, *damn*, he wanted to.

"Rion," Lynx moaned quietly.

Orion didn't know if it was for show or for real, but he felt that little moan all the way to his toes. He threaded his fingers into Lynx's soft hair and tightened his grip. The footsteps came closer, and Lynx went to jump apart, but Orion held him tight so that their faces were squished together. Less visible that way.

"Orion, take it to your room or back to the party. None of your friends are allowed back here. You know that."

It was Aries. Orion chuckled nervously against Lynx's lips.

"C'mon, baby. Let's go to my room," he murmured, adding a bit of a drunken slur to his words. He took Lynx's hand and made sure to turn him so Aries didn't see his face. He wasn't sure if Aries would recognize Lynx, but he wasn't taking any chances.

They tripped along like drunken lovers down the hall,

arms around each other's waists, hands groping. He had to give Lynx credit for picking up on the charade quickly.

Once people were in view they stopped every few feet to kiss or nuzzle each other's necks. Charade or not, Orion's skin was tingling, and the heat in his belly was as real as it got. He was nervous, though. They had to go through the main party to get to the wing that held his bedroom. It was going to be a few tense minutes. He hoped that Lynx had the skills to bluff his way through it.

"You're doing fine. We're going to make our way to the party and then to my room. I'll lock the keypad, so no one will be able to get in. Okay?"

Lynx nodded and then giggled softly, making sure to keep his face at least halfway turned into Orion's neck. Orion was impressed. He knew Lynx had to be scared. Being caught in the Leonias estate would mean more trouble for him than either one of them could explain their way out of, and he doubted that Lynx ever meant to make an actual appearance at the party.

He had to give the guy credit for his acting skills, though. If Orion hadn't known better, he'd have assumed that Lynx was drunk and clingy and dying to get into his pants. Lynx flattened his palm against Orion's abdomen, his pinky straying dangerously low. Orion tipped his head back against Lynx's shoulder, covered the teasing hand with his own, and let his face show how much he wanted more.

"Through that doorway, then we're out of the main room," he murmured, making a show out of biting the edge of Lynx's ear.

He saw a few of his friends give him sly, inebriated smiles. At least no one would be looking for him after he disappeared. Lynx shivered and subtly picked up the pace.

Orion breathed a sigh of relief when they finally got to

the stairwell that led to the family's private wing. The show wasn't over until they were behind a locked door, but it was much safer than it had been in the main room.

He separated himself from Lynx by a few inches but grabbed his hand and pulled him along, trying to look eager instead of nervous, toward safety. When they were there, finally, and the keypad was locked, Orion let out a huge breath and shoved at Lynx's shoulders.

"What the hell were you thinking? My father would *kill* you."

"I don't care."

"Yes, you do. Don't be stupid."

Lynx sighed. "You're right. I do care. But I can't stop thinking about what you're doing, and how much I want to be a part of it. And more than anything," he reached up and cupped Orion's face. "I can't stop wishing I was kissing you. I've missed you." Lynx leaned his forehead against Orion's and sighed. "I'm sure that makes me sound like the biggest loser in the universe, but it's true."

Orion's chest suddenly felt tight, like he couldn't take a full breath. "I've missed you too," he whispered. "A lot. But why? We barely know each other."

"I know," Lynx answered. He gave Orion a tender brushing kiss. "But I want to know more."

Another kiss followed, more lingering. It ended with a soft swipe of Lynx's tongue against Orion's bottom lip. Orion shivered and stepped back. It was so hard to stay rational.

"Were you following me tonight?"

"Yeah. I saw you leave the party. I'd been planning on blending in and trying to get you off on your own. What were you doing way back there?"

Orion wasn't sure if he should tell Lynx. He already

knew Orion was stealing from his own family and the Dragon triad as well, but it seemed so much bigger to be spying. He just wasn't —

"Rion. You can trust me. What's it going to take to make you believe that? I'm exactly who I was before you knew I was my father's son."

"I know," Orion answered quietly.

He didn't honestly believe that Lynx would do anything to cause him harm. Orion walked over to his music system and turned it on, shifting through various folders until he found one that was mostly soft and romantic with a vaguely throbbing beat. It would've been perfect for what everyone assumed they were doing, but it was also good for hiding voices. He didn't want to take any chances.

"Sit." He gestured toward his low bed.

Lynx sat nervously, fiddling with the hem of his sleeve. Orion sat next to him and reached over for his hand. It felt natural to thread their fingers together and squeeze.

"I was looking for something," he started. "Earlier, out in the ruins, I was in the city's main database for building specs and plans, downloading the specs for the new shipping tunnel. I ran across the plans for this house, and I opened them out of curiosity, just to pass time. There was a room in the plans that I've never seen. I want to know what's in that room. It has to exist."

"What do you think it is?"

"I have no idea. I hope something completely innocent, but my family, your family, they're not exactly..."

"The innocent type — which is one of the reasons I came here tonight, other than the fact that I needed to see you."

"What are you talking about?"

"I found something that my family's up to, at least, I

think I did. I hacked into my dad's system; you know, looking for shipping information. I wanted to help you." He gave Orion a sincere smile. "But I found something else. I think I got in further than I meant to. I found files that I don't think even other Dragons know about. The letters ARC kept showing up, and I thought it was something you might want to look into."

"ARC? What's that?"

"I don't know. But it was in there a lot. I think it's actually something real, like a machine or a weapon."

"I've never heard of it before."

"I hadn't either, but it seemed important. I wanted you to know. Rion, I want to help you. I don't know how else to say it."

Orion couldn't help the tightening of his stomach when he thought of them working together, both from temptation and fear.

"Listen, when you go back to look for the missing room, do you want me to go look with you?"

Orion thought for a tense thirty seconds or so then nodded slowly. "I do. We have to wait until everyone passes out, though. It's going to be a few hours. Will you be missed?"

"No. Not until morning. My cousins are covering for me."

"They know you're here?" Orion felt a rush of panic.

"*No.*" Lynx chuckled. "Give me some credit. I made up a story about some romantic tryst. They could tell I was into someone anyway. Might as well use it."

"You're into someone, huh?" Orion grinned, unable to help it.

"Fuck off," Lynx answered with a small smile. "You know I am."

"Me too."

And that was when Orion stopped fighting his desire and simply kissed Lynx, long and deep, with all the passion of that last kiss they'd shared behind his bedroom door days earlier, all the heat of the one they'd just had out in the hallway.

It was better, though, because there wasn't any anger or subterfuge, just the sinking, swirling desire that Orion had felt since the first time Lynx had touched him. He drank in Lynx's taste, inhaled his intoxicating scent, moaned, and tried to get closer, so he could feel every contour of Lynx's body.

"Touch me," he demanded softly, taking Lynx's hand and pushing it under his tunic. Lynx tugged his hand free and threaded it into Orion's hair instead.

"Are you going to push me away again?"

"I don't know." It was an honest answer. He'd seen the Phoenix triad take people down for less than what they were doing. "Us being anywhere near each other is so dangerous."

"You've said that before, and I already told you I don't care. I'm still here."

Orion smiled to himself. He could see it finally. There was a Katana behind Lynx's sweet open face. There was desire, passion, the need to do what was right, for himself and for everybody else. Lynx wasn't going to give up and Orion didn't want him to. He saw that Lynx had dropped his gaze to the floor, his free hand back to fiddling with the fabric of his trousers.

"Hey." Orion bumped against Lynx with his shoulder until he looked up and smiled. "I'm glad you're here."

"Me too."

Orion's grin stretched. "You know, we have time to kill. You wanna stare at the floor for the next few hours?"

Lynx chuckled and tugged on Orion's shirt, pulling him until he toppled over, causing them both to sprawl out on the bed. "Nah. Your floor is nice and all, but I've got something else in mind."

"Yeah?" God, Lynx's laugh was sexy. "What were you thinking?"

"This."

Lynx rolled them over so that he was pressing Orion into the mattress, then he kissed him on the mouth, long and slow, before dragging his lips and teeth down the side of Orion's neck.

"I like this."

Orion's breath caught in his throat. Lynx slipped his hands under the thin silky shirt he'd worn for the party.

"You look gorgeous in this shirt, but I think I like your other clothes better. This doesn't seem like you."

"It's not me. Take it off."

Orion arched his back and sighed when his shirt was gone, discarded to the floor. Lynx took his off as well. Orion couldn't help but reach up and trace his fingers all over Lynx's chest. He loved the defined muscles, not too big but very useful. Very pretty as well. He sat up to meet Lynx in a kiss. The kiss felt different, more honest. He was kissing Lynx, not some anonymous Dragon. It was exactly right.

He slid his thighs open, cradling Lynx's hips between them, and rolled his hips, shuddering at the perfect friction of them rubbing together.

"Wanna be naked with you," Lynx murmured against Orion's lips, tugging on the stretchy fabric of his trousers.

Orion wanted it too, but he couldn't seem to stop kissing. He'd never been so intoxicated by a kiss before, but this was different. He wanted it more, deeper and hotter, endless tasting and touching.

Orion slid his hands down Lynx's back into the waist of his trousers. He found more round muscle there, springy and perfectly shaped. Lynx groaned and renewed his effort to divest them of their pants. This time, Orion let go of the kiss long enough for Lynx to tug his bottoms off his hips and down past his knees and ankles until he was blissfully naked.

"You too," he murmured, helping Lynx until he too had nothing but fair perfect skin covering his body. Lynx sank back between Orion's thighs with a sigh, and the kisses started again. Orion couldn't help wrapping his legs around Lynx's thighs and grinding their growing erections together. The hungry slip and slide, coupled with their breathless gasps and moans, made the heat in Orion's stomach start to bubble.

"Orion?" Lynx was breathless and moaning.

He understood. There was no such thing as enough with them. Orion slid his hands down Lynx's back once again, letting his fingers slip in between to nudge up against Lynx's entrance. Lynx groaned and pushed against Orion's fingers, deepening the touch.

"You like that?"

"Yeah. Feels so good."

"You ever had someone inside you?"

"Only, *ohh*, fingers. But I want to."

Lynx's hips bucked again, alternating between pushing up against Orion's fingers and rubbing their cocks together. Orion loved the lost look on Lynx's face, the passionate way he got so into their kisses, how intimate he made everything feel. Orion couldn't wait to get inside of him someday. But not tonight. He needed to remember how Lynx filled him so perfectly. It had been far too long.

"I want to feel you like that too. But right now, I need you in me. Are you ready?"

"God. *Always.*"

Orion would've chuckled if his body hadn't exploded in waves of lust. He dragged himself to the shelf next to his bed to grab the half-empty bottle of lubricant there. He rose to his knees and poured some in his hand before handing the bottle to Lynx. Lynx knelt there, frozen, watching as Orion prepared himself.

"What?" He finally asked, feeling like he'd done something wrong.

"Nothing," Lynx breathed. "That's just so hot. I had to watch." He shuffled toward Orion, and they met, knee to knee, chest to chest. "How do you want it?"

"Stay there," Orion murmured, and he turned, straddling Lynx's thighs with his calves, back to chest. He leaned his head back against Lynx's shoulder. "Like this."

Orion reached behind him and grasped Lynx's slicked erection, guiding it to his entrance. He sank slowly, on a long moan, until Lynx's thick shaft was buried all the way in him. It was so deep, he could barely breathe from feeling so full. It was exactly what he'd been missing. Lynx wrapped his arms around his waist, and Orion covered Lynx's hands with his own.

"Good?" Lynx asked.

"Amazing."

They started to move, slowly at first, with Lynx licking and biting at the side of Orion's neck. It felt so amazingly good. The constant shivers from the bites, the way every stroke nailed him in the perfect spot. He clutched at Lynx's fingers and groaned.

"Want more?" Lynx whispered roughly.

Orion could only nod.

Lynx picked up the pace, bucking his hips harder into Orion, driving him crazy. He loved that they were so connected, skin slipping against skin, hands linked, Lynx's breath in his ear.

"Love this with you," Lynx murmured. "Never wanna stop."

"Me too."

Orion picked up the pace even more, slamming down to meet every one of Lynx's thrusts. Just the pressure alone, brushing, nudging, grinding against his prostate, made him start spiraling into oblivion.

Frantic for release, he separated his hand from Lynx's and grasped his straining erection. Lynx slipped his hand between Orion's thighs, rubbing behind his balls at the soft spot that would make him lose his mind. He bucked up and cried out one last time as the thundering release plowed through him and out into the air. He was vaguely aware of Lynx shouting out as well and warmth filling him, but he was out spinning in the unseen stars.

It took a while for Orion to open his eyes, even longer before he realized that he was still sitting on Lynx, who had to be squatting in a wretchedly uncomfortable position. He lifted up on shaky legs, then collapsed on the bed and held out his hand to Lynx, who took it and flopped down next to him, right on his stomach.

Lynx came up onto his elbows and kissed Orion's chest, one of his nipples, his collarbone, before rubbing noses with him and dropping a small kiss on his lips.

"You can't push me away again. I don't think I'd be able to survive without this anymore."

Orion chuckled softly and wriggled an arm free so he

could pet Lynx's back. "Not going anywhere." He made a face. "Except for the shower. We're a mess."

"In a minute," Lynx mumbled. Then he reached over and folded Orion's blanket around them and closed his eyes.

***

IT WAS cold in the middle of the night. The house was finally silent, the revelers either passed out in a guest room or safe in their own soft beds. Lynx crept down the hallway outside of Orion's bedroom, keeping his eyes on the swishing sapphire braid in front of him. Orion held his hand up when they reached an intersection in the hallway, but then he motioned that it was okay to go.

They tiptoed across the main ballroom, finally silent and wreathed in shadows, and up a sharply angled staircase that took them to the Phoenix administration offices. Lynx continued to follow silently, until they reached a large set of double doors. Orion cracked one of them open and slipped inside the room, motioning for Lynx to follow. Once inside, he cracked on a small portable light, bright enough for them to see by but not bright enough for someone else to notice it from the outside.

"What are we looking for?"

Orion skimmed the inoffensive-looking room as his eyes adjusted to the light.

"I'm not sure; it's just that according to those plans, there should be another room right on the other side of that wall. There's no door in the hallway, and the screen side of this room should be the outside of the house, but I'm guessing it's not. I can't believe I never noticed before." He looked frustrated with himself.

"Are you in here a lot?"

Orion chuckled sourly. "Yeah, right. My dad would never take me seriously enough to include me in meetings."

"But you're the heir."

"Nah, Aries is. I'll inherit the triad in name, but Aries runs the damn thing. Insulting, but it leaves me open to do what's important. Hey, go out in the hallway and listen. I'm going to tap at the far corner of the room. See if you can hear anything."

"Like what?"

"Extra space? I'm not sure. Just try."

Lynx crept out the double doors and into the hallway. He went all the way to the corner, where the hallway turned to the right — the end of the building, as far as he knew. He heard a quiet tapping and listened closely. It wasn't coming from the other side of the wall, at least not where he was. He shifted to the left, closer to the entrance to the conference room. After about eight feet, he got to where the tapping sound seemed to be coming from. He tapped back quietly before jogging with silent steps back into the conference room.

"It wasn't at the end of the hall. When you were at the corner, the noise was at least eight feet from where it should've been. There has to be something behind this wall."

"So now we figure out how to get to it." Orion grinned, his excitement obvious and contagious.

They searched for long minutes, feeling around the big holoscreen and along the baseboards and corners, hoping to find some part of the wall that didn't belong. When it seemed like there was nowhere else that a button or lever could possibly be, they stood. Orion looked frustrated.

"It's gotta be here. There's no other room in this hallway

that could be used to enter that space. This conference area fills up the whole corner."

Lynx went over to the little projection box while Orion was talking and ran his fingers over it absentmindedly. He'd worked a little with the holograph projectors in school, and the one in the Phoenix conference room seemed familiar. There was the power switch, the programming keys, a knob for focusing, and — *hold on.*

There was another switch, near the bottom and away from the rest of the machine's controls. It was small and unobtrusive. No one would ever notice it, unless they were looking for something off.

"Rion, I think I found it," Lynx whispered.

"What?"

"The way into that room. This switch isn't supposed to be on a holoprojector."

Orion leaned over, his face transforming from frustration to excitement. He reached out and covered Lynx's fingers with his own and gave him a quick happy kiss.

"You want to flip it, or do you want me to do it?"

"What if it's loud?"

"It won't be. Couldn't be much of a secret if it made some big noise every time it opened and closed."

"Then you flip it." Lynx grinned at Orion in the semi-darkness.

Orion flipped the switch in the opposite position. At first, nothing happened, but then the holoscreen started to roll up into the ceiling. What at first appeared to be a tiny crack in the wall turned into a door that slid noiselessly open to reveal what was indeed a small room, filled to the brim with row after row of servers and a computer screen mounted onto the wall. An impressive array of machinery sat below it -- not the antique mishmash that Orion worked with out in the ruins, but new and top of the line.

Orion ran his fingers over the servers, as if he couldn't quite believe they were there. "There's gotta be years worth of info in these things."

"Yeah, and pretty important stuff if it has to be hidden back here."

"I'm going to take a quick look through the servers and see what there is to see."

Orion sat at the main access console and powered up the system. The computer beeped softly as it warmed up. Then Orion expertly tapped in a series of commands that brought up the files of the first, and largest, of the servers.

"The stuff on here is *really* old. From before we were born, for sure."

He was scrolling through the files, reading the names off. There were files named for each of the triads — Dragon, Fox, Hydra, the long-gone Chimera Triad. It made Lynx's mind spin to think of the information that had been gathered over so many years. Then the files turned to financial data, then acquisitions — documents on the many things that the Phoenix triad owned.

"Wait, what's that?" Lynx pointed to a file on the screen. It said ARC.

Orion stopped and scrolled back to the top of the page. "Hey, isn't that the word you said you kept seeing in your dad's files?"

Lynx nodded. Orion opened the file and immediately they were shown a page of complicated schematics and engineering drawings.

"It looks like a machine, a weapon maybe? It's hard to tell without studying it." Orion tapped in a few more commands and ran a search through all the servers, using the key word ARC. It came up with hundreds of files, the list filling the screen and then some.

"Holy shit, what *is* this thing? And even more, why do both of our families have so much information about it?" Lynx murmured in wonder.

"You know what? I think I'm going to send a copy of these files to our system out in the ruins. There's no way we're going to be able to slog through all of this right here. I'll just have to open a portal so it doesn't take forever to load."

"And you can get rid of the evidence that the portal was there?"

Lynx was treated to an exaggerated eye roll. "Who am I?"

"Yeah, yeah."

"After I do this, we need to get you out of here. We've tempted fate long enough."

"The fate tempting felt pretty amazing earlier, didn't it?"

Orion trembled a little bit at the memory. "You know it did."

He'd opened a portal and was busily sending the files through it to the computer out in the ruins. Lynx couldn't wait to get into them and see what this ARC thing was all about.

"When are we going to look at these?"

Orion raised his eyebrows. "We?"

"Yeah. You're not going to leave me hanging on this. That name was in nearly every file in this system and in my own. I've gotta know what's going on. Besides, I'm your inside Dragon guy. If this involves both of the triads, you need me."

Orion flashed him a smile. "Can you get away tomorrow?"

Lynx didn't care what was happening at the Dragon complex the next day; he'd be wherever Orion was. "Yeah."

"Then why don't you meet me at the storage shed at one, and I'll take you over to our new place. It's not as big, but at least it's a little warmer."

Lynx grinned as the computer beeped, signaling the end of the file transfer. Orion went into a few folders and deleted the evidence of the file transfer, than opened the main logbook for the computer and erased the fact that they'd ever there in the first place. After that, they shut the computers down and slipped out, closing the wall to the secret office room behind them and putting the holoscreen back into place.

"TOMORROW," Lynx whispered at the back entrance to the Leonias house that Orion had taken him to.

He leaned over and nipped at Orion's lips. Lynx didn't want to say good night. He wanted to sprawl in bed naked with Orion at his side, where he could touch him whenever he wanted. It was frustrating to go home alone. Orion answered the nip with a soft swipe of his tongue.

"Tomorrow. Mmm, I don't want to let you go." He pushed at Lynx's chest, though, in an effort to send him on his way.

"I don't want to go either. Let's just go to the ruins together now. I wanna be with you again."

Orion chuckled. "I need to show my face in the morning. I'm probably going to get a lecture from my parents on propriety. I'm sure they've already heard about that little show we put on."

Lynx cringed. "Sorry."

"It's okay. Turned out to be more than worth it."

Lynx shivered at the soft touch to his jaw and the kiss that followed it.

"Go now, before I end up taking you back upstairs and getting you killed when my family finds out you're here."

Lynx nodded and backed away, turning to start the short walk to his family's estate. "I'll see you tomorrow," he called softly.

"Tomorrow," Orion echoed with a wave

Chapter Nine

LYNX SLIPPED out of his family's Cloud Level compound and into the lift that would take him all the way down to the murky steam of Bottom City.

He tried to stay calm, pushing down the excitement in his stomach. Lynx knew he had a long dangerous walk to get out to the ruins, and the last thing anyone wanted to do was become complacent in Bottom City. That was the best way he knew of to get killed.

It was hard not to get excited, though. He felt like he'd been in the starting blocks all morning, waiting nervously for another chance to see Orion, wanting to know what the machine was that both his and Orion's families were somehow connected to.

When the lift hit ground and he exited into the newly familiar noise and chaos of Bottom City, Lynx's excitement grew.

Just get to the tunnel. Don't look at anyone.

He kept his hand on his pistol and looked around surreptitiously. Unlike the morning when he'd been taken unawares, now he used every drop of the training he'd received as a triad member to access his surroundings.

It seemed his precautions were unnecessary; the citizens of the bottom were bustling around, pale and mouse-like, ignoring his presence. It didn't seem like a very long time at all until he was in the basement with the crates, slipping into the tunnel that would lead him to the ruins.

The tunnel was as dark and cramped as it had been the first time he was in it, but he felt considerably more comfortable, like he was meant to be in it, meant to be sneaking out to the ruins to meet with Orion, meant to be —

He stopped, frozen, when he heard a light scuffling sound a ways down the tunnel. Instinctively, Lynx drew back into the shadows of the already dark tunnel and put his hand on his pistol, ready to draw it.

"I know it's you. You can stop hiding. Oh, and please don't shoot me. That would be annoying."

There was a hint of laughter in the very familiar voice. Lynx sighed out his tension and stepped into the middle of the tunnel.

"You scared the crap out of me. I thought I was going to have to kill someone."

"Nope." Orion reached him and immediately curled his hand around Lynx's neck to draw him in for a kiss.

"This isn't the storage shed," Lynx murmured against Orion's lips with a slow smile. He couldn't get used to how soft and amazing Orion's lips felt on his own.

"I know. I got impatient." The side of Orion's mouth tipped in a self-deprecating smile.

Lynx trailed his fingers down Orion's arm to twine their fingers together. "I'm glad. Ready to go look at those files?"

Orion nodded and tugged on Lynx's hand.

· · ·

HOURS LATER, they were surrounded by screens all showing different variations on the same thing. A machine that from what they could tell from the blueprints and files made...*air?*

"But that's stupid," Lynx said for what felt like the millionth time. "Why would anyone want a machine that made air? And if they did have it, what was with all the hidden files?"

"I have no idea." Orion looked just as perplexed as he was. They needed more answers, but there was just so much information. It would take months to go through it all. "There has to be more to this."

"Yeah, but what?"

Lynx returned his gaze to the screen he was working on and scrolled down through the files that he'd made a copy of from the Dragon house.

He was scanning through his own family's files on the mysterious machine while Orion looked through the Phoenix files on the same thing. In his system alone there were nearly a hundred folders stuffed with schematics, plans, directions for operation. It seemed pretty boring, if Lynx was honest.

Until he saw something that caught his interest.

"Hey wait, here's something that says 'contract.' Maybe it's the original, you know, for building the machine." Lynx tapped on the folder, opening it.

Inside was one lone document. Orion stood from where he'd been working and came behind Lynx, draping his arms around Lynx's shoulders and kissing his neck.

"What is it?"

Lynx was reading the document intently, his face becoming more and more concerned with every line he read.

"This is a contract between The Dragons and The Phoenixes, nearly seventy years ago. It says that they went in on contracting the ARC together and goes on to list all of the secrecy measures that both triads would take to ensure the existence of the machine would never be revealed to anyone else, not even lower triad members. It looks like only the leaders know the thing even exists. Hey, and look, it says that ARC stands for something." Lynx enlarged the print on the screen. "Atmospheric Regulation Computer. What the—"

"You said the contract was signed seventy years ago? The Dragons and The Phoenixes weren't even in power at that point."

"Yeah, but they were soon after, within a couple of years, actually. That's when all of the pharmaceutical companies first opened, and both of our families slowly rose in the ranks."

"Guess you were paying attention in school," Orion teased. Lynx chuckled and lifted his lips for a small kiss.

"Good thing someone was. Anyway, it all has to be connected somehow. I mean, they make this machine together, and within a few short years, two relatively small and unimportant triads are in charge of the entire city."

Orion suddenly had a queasy look on his face.

"Hey, what's the matter?"

"Lynx, when did the sky above the old city go black?"

It was part of their heritage, ingrained in their histories. But most kids in their position didn't think about it often. After all, life in cloud city with its simulated sky and perfectly temperate air didn't exactly lead any of them to care much about the darkness outside.

Lynx's eyes widened. "You don't think they would —"

But he knew that was wrong. From what he knew of

both his and Orion's fathers, there was nothing they wouldn't do to stay in power.

"Wasn't the permanent cloud supposedly tied to the Sphinx-Chimera conflict? Damage from the battle or something?"

"That's when the old city was ruined. The sky has been black --" Lynx paused and choked a little. "It's been black since right before our parents were born. A little more than sixty years. It was originally blamed on the conflict, but they've since decided that it was slow accumulation of pollutants. Too many for the environment to clean itself. They just gathered into what we have now."

They both stared at the contract silently for long minutes, contemplating the enormity of what it seemed that their families had done.

"It only took a few years to develop the drugs that combat the pollution and the lack of light."

"Which they sold to the highest bidder," Orion supplied. "All of a sudden, our families were rich and in charge of the city."

The two of them were speechless for long minutes. Lynx was having a hard time getting his head around it. Not the war, not the ruins, but everything else was his family's fault. His and Orion's. He almost wished he didn't know.

"So it's all about money and power? They were willing to ruin *everything* for money and power," he finally whispered.

Lynx didn't know what else to say. He'd never been deluded; he knew the triads did some very illegal things, but he couldn't even fathom how they justified that machine. Or the use of it.

"It worked, didn't it?" Orion's voice was quiet and sad.

"The pharmaceuticals are what made them rich, it's what made them what they are today. If there was no pollution, they'd probably still be bowing down to the Sphinxes."

"But if they're in this together, why the fighting?"

Orion shrugged. "Money and power, right? Isn't that what everything is always about? Whoever's the one with the most gets to rule everything, right?"

Lynx nodded. "I guess so. Listen, we need to find proof. Right now, all we have is a theory. We need someone who can look at this information and make sure we're right, make sure that we have clear evidence that's written down and irrefutable."

"Then what?" Orion seemed overwhelmed.

"Then we find the fucking thing and take it down."

Orion laughed softly and leaned on Lynx. "I knew there was a rebel in you," he whispered against Lynx's ear.

***

"TOMORROW'S GOING to be fine, you know." Lynx dragged a kiss across Orion's sweaty forehead.

They had snuck into Orion's private room at the Phoenix bar long after the main crowd had gone home. Lynx had his lover's warm pliable body strewn across him, and he was running seeking fingers up and down the indents in Orion's damp spine.

It had taken nearly two days, but with Pavo's help, they'd finally tracked down the information that proved their worst theories correct. There was a machine, hidden up in Cloud Level, that was producing the toxic chemicals that polluted the sky in amounts too overwhelming for any natural force to effectively clean them out of its system.

It made sense. With the wind from the ocean, New Seattle would've been clear of the cloud decades before, had it been natural.

It took even longer to figure out where the machine was hidden. After that, all they had to do was come up with a plan to destroy it.

They didn't want any explosions, or fires —nothing that would announce their presence, since it turned out the machine was hidden in plain sight on one of the major boulevards on Cloud Level.

Pavo and Orion worked out a way to disconnect it and damage the parts to the point where the thing wouldn't be able to be put back together without being totally rebuilt. It would be one big useless hunk of metal, which would take too long to replace before the cloud cover dissipated. They hoped. All that was left was for the plan to work.

And it had to work.

"Fine?" Orion choked on a laugh. "Are you in denial?"

Lynx tugged his hair. "No, but there's no point in being defeatist."

"I do hope everything goes well tomorrow," Orion murmured tiredly. "It kind of has to. That feels nice, you know," he added. "I love the way you touch me."

Lynx made a happy mumbling noise and continued to trace invisible patterns on Orion's back. "I want to be inside of you," he finally murmured.

"Again?" Orion sighed and pretended to roll his eyes but then he grinned and wiggled up to straddle Lynx's hips. He stroked Lynx's still slick shaft until it hardened and shifted so that he could sink down onto it. Orion let out a satisfied little grunt, then leaned forward to drop smacking little kisses on Lynx's lips. "Better?"

"Yeah." Lynx smiled, tucking Orion's hair behind his ear and cupping his face, unable to believe how important he'd become in just a few short weeks. "I —"

"Shhhh, just love me."

He rolled his hips then and started to move, threading their fingers together like he always did. Orion moaned and shivered when Lynx hit his prostate. He was trembling and grinding as close to Lynx as he could get.

"How can it be so good every time?" Lynx mumbled hoarsely. He shuddered and tightened his fingers on Orion's.

He wanted to grab Orion's hips, grip his ass, run his fingers over the pale graceful cock that was bouncing right in front of his face, but he knew Orion wouldn't let go of his fingers.

"Just is. You sure...*ohhh*...talk a lot."

Lynx grinned at Orion and angled his hips, pumping again and again against Orion's prostate. They tried to draw it out, but that never seemed to work very well. It simply felt too good to last long. Lynx felt the start of Orion's orgasm pulsing around him. Orion threw his head back and moaned. The combination of Orion's exquisite beauty and the hot throbbing heat surrounding him made Lynx lose it, pouring everything he had left into the warmth of Orion's body.

They lay boneless for long minutes, slick and tired and hot, fingers drifting across skin, breathing slowing down. Eventually, though, Orion sat up, clearly reluctant to let reality intrude.

"We'd better go. It's going to be morning soon, and neither of us can afford to get noticed today."

Lynx nodded. "Meet at the new place?"

"Yes. After dinner. We've gotta make sure it happens tonight, in case anyone on either of our sides notices that someone was snooping in their files."

Lynx crawled from the bed and started pulling on his clothes but got distracted by watching Orion, pale, lithe, and beautiful, do the same. He felt a small ache in his chest.

"I wish I could fall asleep holding you."

Orion gave him a small smile. "Me too, but not tonight. C'mon. Let's go."

IT WAS JUST GOING to be the two of them, Lynx and Orion.

The others weren't from the highest level of the Cloud City complex like they were and wouldn't have as good of an excuse to be up there.

Besides, Orion felt like this was their mission. It was their families who'd built the damn thing in the first place. The poetic justice of him and Lynx being the ones to take it out seemed to be perfect.

Pavo had given him a bitter little disappointed look when Orion explained his reasoning, but he figured Pavo would get over it. There would be other operations on other days. Orion had no illusion that ruining one machine would get rid of the monsters that the Phoenix and Dragon triads had become — and family or not, the triads needed to be destroyed.

LYNX AND ORION waited in the ruins, running over their plans again and again, until they were sure that Cloud City would be deserted, all the good little citizens asleep in their beds. Orion mused that if it was a book, like the old ones he used to read in the library, it would say that the heroes waited for the cover of darkness.

It made him grin to think that maybe, if they were successful and didn't get killed trying, then some day soon that saying could be used again. Because there would be darkness, but more importantly, there would be light. Real light. It seemed impossible to believe.

The walk through the tunnel seemed to take about a tenth of the time it usually did. He was nervous, of course. Of all the crazy-ass stunts he'd pulled off since he'd donned the robe of Katana, this one was the most impossible.

In theory, it should've been no problem. Get to the ugly old sculpture right outside the amphitheater in the middle of Cloud Level's public square, find the circuitry to disable it, burn the wires and the seventy-year-old motherboard, and it should be done. The sky would clear before the triads could fix the antique parts.

That was the theory at least.

In reality, it was going to be dangerous, right out in the open, and once they started disassembling the monster, there would be no way to hide what they were doing from anyone who may happen to see. Orion hoped desperately that nobody would see, that they'd be able to get out of there with none the wiser.

They slipped out of the tunnels and made it without incident to the private, unrecorded lift that originated right behind the Phoenix club. It was best not to have one of the public lifts mark their passage that night. On the lift ride up to the clouds, Orion's stomach fluttered queasily. He usually got a bit of nerves before any major operation, but now he felt downright nauseated.

"Lynx, what if something goes wrong?" Orion wanted

to gag. He couldn't believe something that insecure had just slipped out of his mouth.

Lynx moved closer and wrapped his arms around Orion, pulling him close. It felt good to be held, as much as he hated to admit it. Lynx brought out everything that was soft and needy in him.

"We're gonna be fine, Rion. I hope. And if we're not, well, I'm still not sorry. What we're doing is the most important thing to happen in this city in more than half a century. It'll happen silently in the middle of the night, but it'll change so many lives."

"I know. I don't know what my problem is. I'm not usually like this."

"Hey, I'm scared too. Scared to death. It would be stupid to go into this, thinking that it's no problem. What's that old line? It's only brave if you're scared but you still do it anyway? Something like that. Rion, you're the bravest person I know."

The lift slowed, and its doors slipped noiselessly open. Orion took a deep fortifying breath.

"Okay. I'm good. Let's do this."

THE ARC STOOD in the middle of the most public of public areas in Cloud Level disguised as modern art. A monster of metal and hidden circuitry, it had been 'donated' to the city ages ago by the Dragon and Phoenix triads during a time of civic rejuvenation after the Sphinx-Chimera Conflict. There was even a nice little plaque at the base, proclaiming the two triads as 'Patrons of the Arts.' Orion snorted quietly at the irony. Such bullshit.

The thing looked like a monster to him, a symbol of

everything that was wrong with New Seattle. He could still barely believe that if he and Lynx were successful, then the pollution, however slowly, would disappear and there would be *sky* again. No matter how logically he knew the truth, he couldn't believe that for sure his father, and maybe others in his family, knew about the machine and, for money alone, let it go on, blackening the sky.

No more.

Orion pulled out the blast pistol that he'd turned on high. He motioned for Lynx to circle around to the back of the sculpture so he could start cutting through to the inside, while he took watch.

The machine's access panel was disguised in a curve of the abstract sculpture, which Orion and his friends had always referred to as 'butt ugly mountain.' It rose from the central green in Cloud Level's public square all the way to the top of the glass dome above it. Orion imagined that it actually probably rose through the glass, but it was nearly impossible to tell from the ground. He nodded at Lynx, who withdrew his own weapon to start disabling the machine. Zinging heat and sparks filled the air when Lynx turned his blast pistol on to the highest stream and started cutting through the thick bolts that secured the hidden panel. Orion's heart beat, faster and harder with every pinging drop of yet another bolt.

"Orion."

He heard Lynx whisper his name after a few tense minutes punctuated only by the faint roar of Lynx's laser pistol and the metallic clank of bolts hitting the ground. Orion breathed deep. It had seemed like a million bolts had fallen before Lynx was finally done.

He jogged around to the other side of the sculpture,

scanning the dark square for people. The place, thankfully, still seemed deserted. He stood, ready to grab the panel and lower it quietly once the last bolt was removed.

The panel came off surprisingly easily after the bolts were removed. Orion would've expected more of a fight, since the thing had likely been stuck together for years at a time. The machinery looked slightly different on the inside than they had in the pictures on the computer. It had been repaired a few times, obviously, with newer pieces that didn't quite fit. Orion thought that maybe it would even make their job easier. The thing was practically stuck together with chewing gum.

"Lynx, pull the blue input wires. I'm going to start smashing the circuits on the motherboard."

Lynx gave him a tight nod, and they both got to work on the tasks they planned to execute back at the ruins, slowly deconstructing the machine to the point that it would be nearly impossible to ever be put back together again.

Orion picked through the massive wiring system until he had a clean view of the motherboard. Once that thing was smashed, it would be nearly impossible to repair. Any new processor would never fit in or work with the ancient wires. They'd have to rebuild the whole thing.

Orion was banking on the fact that the triads wouldn't be able to pull it off before the pollution had dissipated and the people discovered what had happened.

He could almost feel the thing dying as he started smashing the circuitry on the board while Lynx tugged on the main wires until they were hanging, like dead snakes, from the open repair panel.

Lynx pulled and Orion smashed, piece by piece, bit by bit, until the machine finally groaned and went silent. The faint whirring that Orion had never even noticed other than as part of the general background noise of Cloud Level stopped, and there was utter and complete silence across the yawning darkness of the indoor park.

They'd killed the beast. It was dead.

All that was left was to destroy the parts so it couldn't be put back together again. They had a huge pile of wires at their feet and were getting ready to melt the last of the old circuit board when there was a loud scuffle behind them.

"Hands up!" A voice shouted.

"Aries," Orion whispered, panicking and turning to run, but it was too late. A light shone in his face, clear as day.

"Orion? What the *hell* are you doing here?" He could hear the shock in his cousin's voice.

"I told you I'd give you Katana." A cold clear voice carried through the darkness.

The last person Orion ever expected to see sauntered into the beam of the flashlight. He was smiling, wearing new clothes and sporting a brand-new expensive haircut.

"Pavo?" Orion could only whisper hoarsely. His voice sounded weak and shocked. He *felt* weak and shocked.

Pavo tilted his chin up and raised his eyebrows. "What, did you still expect me follow you around like a fucking dog after you replaced me with that Dragon kid?"

He looked at Orion like he should've known better.

"I gave you *so* many chances to bring me tonight instead of him. This really is your doing." He shook his head slowly, as if he were exasperated with Orion's poor choices. "Oh well. I work for someone new now -- he actually pays me. Oh, and by the way, Aries, there's your accomplice, the Dragon kid that you thought was Katana. He's just some poor dumb fool Orion was fucking. He's fucked now, all right."

Pavo laughed softly at his own joke. Everyone else stared, shocked and silent.

"Pavo, why?"

Pavo raised his eyebrows instead and shook his head. *Stupid moron*, Orion chastised himself. He'd *trusted* Pavo.

"I told you why. I wasn't getting replaced by *that*." He pointed disdainfully at Lynx.

Orion didn't know why he asked. It didn't matter why, all that mattered was that it was done, and he and Lynx were dead. Fuck if he wasn't going to go down fighting, though. He crouched, ready to move.

Out of nowhere, it seemed, the room broke into chaos. Everyone who'd been standing stock-still and tense burst into action. Orion spun and slid to the floor at the same time as one of Aries' men took out a pistol and shot it at him. Aries shoved the man aside at the same time as Lynx also ducked to the floor. Aries and his other backup came sprinting toward Orion and Lynx.

There's no way to run fast enough. Shit.

Orion's cousin was running, drawing closer with every short second. He waved his arm at Lynx, trying to get through. Lynx understood. In the last moments before Aries and his men were on them, Lynx took aim with his blast pistol and melted what was left of the machine's motherboard. Then he aimed at the pile of wires and blasted them with a ray of intense heat until the air was filled with the sulfurous smell of burning plastic and dust.

Then Lynx's gun was kicked out of his hand, and he was cuffed and dragged from the ground. Orion felt cuffs being slammed onto his own wrists, and he was pulled from the floor to stand next to Lynx.

We're dead, but we did it. We did it.

The heart and veins of the old machine were smoldering and dying, impossible to regenerate.

"Let me take the son of a bitch. He's my family. The other one too. I'll meet you guys at the holding cells."

"But Aries." His second in command looked concerned. "That's not following protocol. Plus, there are two of them."

"I'll be fine," Aries barked. "Just get to the detention center and get the interrogation room ready. Oh, and toss this little asshole back down to Metrolevel, where he belongs."

Pavo looked aghast. "But Aries, I thought I was working with you now."

"You were. And now you're not." He shrugged. "Besides, why would I want someone on my team who informs on his leader? You're scum. Take the money, and get out of my face. Be glad I don't kill you for what you already know — and be sure I will if you even open your mouth once. You don't have my cousin looking out for you anymore."

Pavo's face fell, and he glanced at Orion, perhaps in hopes of pity or comfort. Orion looked away.

Because of you, asshole, Lynx and I are going to be killed as traitors. You expect sympathy? Fuck off.

He glanced at Lynx instead, hoping to make some sort of connection. Lynx looked up and gave him a tiny sad smile.

'*We did it,*' he mouthed. Orion nodded.

They were led away by Aries to one of the smaller hallways that headed toward the Phoenix detention center. As they trudged along the hallway, closer and closer to their doom, Orion's heart began to pound.

Maybe my father won't kill me. I'm his son, after all.

Maybe he'll just make me disappear. But they'd kill Lynx for sure. God, I can't let that happen.

With every step, he became more agitated.

He was shocked when his restrainer cuffs suddenly dropped to the floor.

"Punch me," Aries said, his voice harsh. "Punch me and run like hell. You were never part of this, and I never want to see your face up here again."

Wait, *what?* For the second time that night, Orion was in shock. Aries was letting him go? But no, he wasn't going to run without Lynx. He could never be that kind of a coward.

"Aries, you gotta let Lynx go. I was in charge of the whole thing. He's only been around for a few days. You heard Pavo. My father might not kill me. Lynx is dead for sure if dad gets his hands on him."

"Don't be an idiot, Orion. I'm letting *you* go. I'll get my prisoner, and I won't have to kill my family. Take it or leave it. You've got about thirty seconds until the deal expires and you go down with your pretty Dragon boyfriend."

Orion took it — that and a whole lot more.

He pulled back and whaled on Aries as hard as he could, taking his cousin who'd always vastly underestimated him by surprise. Then, knowing Aries was never going to let Lynx go, he grabbed the pistol from Aries's holster and knocked him over the head hard enough to put him out for at least a few minutes. Then he pushed the remote for Lynx's restrainer cuffs, and they dropped to the ground.

"*Run,*" he whispered forcefully. Lynx looked at him, shocked, then he suddenly realized what was going on and turned to bolt. "Lynx, this way."

Orion pointed him to a cramped stairwell, the door barely visible in the wall. They slammed down the back stairwell, heading down and down and down in tight spirals, the walls a constant blur of dirty white only broken by meaningless numbered doors. They ran for what seemed like ages, until Orion saw a number that he thought might be low enough to be safe.

"Here, through this doorway. We should be in Metrolevel by now."

They cracked the doorway open and saw that they were indeed in Metrolevel — in one of the service hallways of the big sports stadium.

"We should take the public lift," Lynx said. "Who cares if it records us? Your private lift is too far."

"You're right, plus I can't go near any Phoenix property again. Public lift it is."

They ran lightly toward the large bank of lifts that serviced the arena. The arena's lifts didn't go all the way to the bottom, but the lift would get them far enough. They'd be able to switch lifts and ride to the bottom. Once they were in the lift, and relatively safe, Orion sagged against the wall.

"We've gotta move tonight. Take only what we can carry and destroy the rest."

Lynx nodded. "You have somewhere in mind?"

"I always have somewhere in mind. I'm paranoid like that."

"Hey, it's not paranoia if they're really after you."

Orion chuckled but thought to himself how weird it was that they were having what felt like a regular conversation after what they'd just been through.

"Hey, Orion," Lynx said after they'd been quiet for a moment or two.

"Yeah?"

"You were pretty amazing tonight. Thanks for saving me from your cousin."

"You were pretty amazing yourself. You're the one who took the machine out."

"We both did. Together."

Orion nodded and slipped his hand into Lynx's as the Midtown lift stopped at the bottom of its route.

"HEY, YOU," Lynx muttered softly as a sleepy Orion woke and turned to curl his body around Lynx's.

They were out in the ruins, resting on a soft air mattress that had been jammed into the corner of their latest hide-out, the only place where either of them would be safe after what'd happened only a few hours ago.

"Hey," Orion replied and wriggled up until his lips could brush against Lynx's.

"I still can't believe it worked. We won. By the skin of our teeth, maybe, but we won."

Orion winced and sighed. "We won the battle, barely, but not the war. Not for a long time. And Pavo. I still can't believe it."

"I'm really sorry about him. I know you trusted him."

"I thought we were friends. I was such an idiot."

"No, you're just a good person, and you thought he was too." Lynx hugged Orion, squeezing just to make sure he could still feel him there. "That doesn't make you an idiot.

He squeezed Orion again and smiled when Orion wriggled closer and sighed contentedly in the darkness, reaching out to hold Lynx's hand. They stayed that way for long minutes, twining and untwining their fingers, nuzzling against each other for comfort.

"Rion?" Lynx's whisper echoed, surprising in the dark.

"Yeah."

"You know I'm falling in love with you, don't you?"

Orion pushed himself up on his elbows, his sapphire hair pooling on the ground on either side of Lynx's face. He squeezed his eyes shut.

"Oh, God, it's such a bad idea. I mean, the danger, with what we already have to do everyday. Especially now."

"Are we back there again? How many times do I have to tell you that I don't care?" Lynx heard the stubbornness in his voice — he meant it too. Orion made him happy, even in the middle of the mess they'd gotten themselves into. He didn't even want to consider letting Orion go. Lynx lifted his face to rub noses with Orion. "I'm not letting you go, okay?"

Orion closed his eyes for a moment, then shifted so one hand was free to trace little patterns on Lynx's face. He looked at Lynx for long silent moments, his eyes lost in thought. Finally he spoke, his voice quiet.

"I think I've been falling in love with you since that first night when we barely said a word to each other. I want to be with you. I just don't know how it can possibly work. What we've gotten ourselves into is going to be a fight, a long one, and I'm not willing to give up on taking down the triads. Can we survive that?"

Lynx lifted his head again to give Orion a soft kiss. "I think together is the only way that we *will* survive."

"So we fight...together?"

"Yes. We fight together. You and me."

Orion nodded tiredly and kissed Lynx once again before letting his body slump down until it was resting, sleep-heavy and sweet, on top of him. Lynx closed his eyes then and let himself relax. His head was comfortable against the soft plush fabric; his body was tired and ready to fall back into oblivion.

Lynx knew he had to be imagining it, it was far too soon for any real change, but as he drifted off with his arms around Orion, he could've sworn that he felt the first warming rays of the sun.

About the Author

MJ O'Shea has never met a music festival, paintbrush, or flower crown she can stay away from. She loves rainstorms and a perfect cup of tea, beach days, music, bright colors, and more than anything a cozy evening with a really great book.

She is from the Pacific Northwest. While she still lives there and loves it, MJ has the heart of a wanderer. So she puts all her dreams of far off places and extraordinary people in her books.

Except for every once in a while when she does what all travelers have to do on occasion... come home.